A Little Something for Everyone

A Little Something for Everyone

Stories, Monologues, Dialogues, & Observations

by KATE KASTEN

ISLET PRESS · IOWA CITY

BY THE SAME AUTHOR

Too Happy

Better Days

The Deconversion of Kit Lamb

Ten Small Beds

Foreign Ground: Stories

Wildwood: Fairy Tales and Fables Re-imagined

Islet Press, Iowa City
www.katekasten.com
ISBN: 978-0-578-68345-4
Cover design by Will Thomson
Typeset by Sara T. Sauers

ENCOURAGED BY the irresistible *Schott's Original Miscellany*, a book of haphazard facts and statistics, most of which you don't need to know and only some of which you will remember, I have put together this collection of random stories, monologues, dialogues and observations.

From the satirical to the serious, from two pages to forty-two and without any discernible theme, the pieces in this book give you no idea of what's coming next. You'll just have to turn the page.

Contents

Conscience

THE CHILD SAT on the sofa with a book open in her lap. She wasn't so much reading the book as staring into it, her lips meeting in a thin tense line. It was early evening in late July. The house was quiet, for a change. Her father and little brother had gone away on an errand in the car. The old spaniel, its muzzle hanging over the top step, was cooling off on the porch. In the next room, the child's mother sat repairing a lamp at the dining room table. Intermittently, the mother hummed a meandering tune.

For a while the child had lain propped against a cushion on the sofa, holding the book close to her face as if willing the story to carry her away from her thoughts, but at last she lowered the book and pulled herself upright, as upright as was possible. At not quite eight years old, she already seemed to walk around with a weight across her small stooped shoulders.

Finally, the silent harassment of her thoughts won out, and she let the pages fall shut in her lap. Sounds issued from the dining room: the snip of a wire, the wooden chair scraping as her mother moved closer to her task, the nameless tune her mother hummed. With each sound the girl's heart fluttered. She folded her arms tightly across her middle to push down the lump of dread that weighed there.

At any moment her mother would finish with the lamp, her

brother and father would come home, and the opportunity to unburden herself would be lost once again. Now—while all was quiet and her mother was alone—this was the time to do the thing she knew she must do sooner or later, yet she found it impossible to detach herself from the sofa and take those few steps into the next room.

Earlier in the afternoon, she and her little brother had chased each other about the orchard, picked green apples and taken turns tossing them for the old spaniel to retrieve and drool over at their feet. They joked and giggled together until dinner time.

At the dinner table, the little girl had at first eaten with a fair appetite: corn-on-the-cob from their garden, slices of cold sweet tomatoes that she cut into finicky pieces, a bit of ham with the fat taken off, and half a slice of bread.

Her father announced, "It looks as if I'm getting that raise in salary, but don't anyone talk about it yet. It's confidential."

The girl found she was suddenly unable to finish her food.

"What's 'a raisin saralee'?" her little brother asked, making her parents smile. The mother held up a glass of water in a toast.

Now from the next room came the sound of a tool being set down on the table and the cane seat creaking as her mother rose. The little girl leaned forward, pressing on her knees with clammy palms. Her mother's footsteps tapped briskly on the tile. The swinging door to the kitchen brushed open and back. A cupboard door squeaked and then closed. Her mother's footsteps returned. She caught a glimpse of her walking past the open doorway with a light bulb in one hand, then heard the sound of the bulb being screwed in, the lamp being plugged into the wall, a click, another click, her mother's puzzled "huh." The little girl could picture the mild frown that would crease her forehead as she set to work again.

Now, the child thought. She had put off this moment so often before, and she was so weary of the burden she carried, that she felt a moment of eagerness almost, but in another moment a voice said, *No, never mind. You can do it tomorrow.* Her familiar tempter, the one who had kept her in this agonizing suspense for so long, always presented a convincing case. This time it said, "If you don't finish your book tonight, you won't be able to take it back to the library in the morning, and you'll only get to check out five new ones instead of six."

This was a good argument, for she was an avid, greedy reader. She glanced down at the book open beside her. In it, there was a girl of about her age who convinced her farmer father to spare the life of a runt pig. The girl was so patient and trustworthy that animals spoke in her presence. The child wanted to be brave and determined like her.

With this admirable character fresh in her mind, she came to a decision. *Now*, she said, under her breath. *I'm going to do it now.* And she began to rise from the sofa.

Just then, a sound from the porch stopped her from completing the action; her brother and father were returning already. It wouldn't be possible for her to make this confession in front of them. With a cold, dull feeling of relief, she lowered herself back down.

But the sound turned out after all to be the dog rising and shaking himself. His claws clicked across the wood floor as he came to stand beside her. He placed his chin on her knee and gazed up at her with twitching eyebrows and the sad, anxious expression produced by the rolls of loose skin on his forehead. She stroked him, confused by the fast shifts of her emotions, the dread and guilt, then the disappointment and relief, and—already creeping back again—fear.

If only the others *had* come back! By now they had probably finished filling the car with gas and were stopping at the supermarket to get milk for breakfast. They would pick up the gingersnaps for a treat before bedtime, and by the time they got home they would have opened the box of cookies and enjoyed one or two of them in the car together. Her little brother would burst through the door with several of them in his outstretched hands. "Three cookies for you," he would say, "and one more for me. I had two already." He always shared things with her.

The dog would nose around them, swishing his feathery tail in anticipation of the crumbs they would let him lick off their hands, and for the hundredth time she would lose her courage.

It calmed her somewhat to comb her fingers through the thick curls on the dog's shoulders. The dog clunked down on the carpet and gave a mournful sigh. The child looked up at the ticking clock, wishing it said nine o'clock instead of eight o'clock. If it were nine o'clock, she would be in bed now, listening to her mother softly picking out a sonatina from the practice book on the big upright piano that stood at the bottom of the stairs. She would fall asleep to her mother's dainty notes drifting up the stairwell and her father's thin offkey voice humming along.

All at once she knew she was going to do it this time, the way a person in a burning building knows when the heat of the fire has become more intolerable than the fear of jumping. Weakly, like the invalid boy in her favorite story about the secret garden, she pulled herself to the edge of the sofa and dragged herself to her feet.

It was getting dark in the dining room, with a pink tinge of sunset through the windows. Her mother had been so absorbed in her task that she had forgotten to turn on the overhead light. The child didn't turn it on for her as she ordinarily would have—imitating her father's "Let's get some light on the subject!"—but stood by the doorway without saying anything. Behind the table where her mother sat, three west-facing windows framed the trees in the orchard. Their elongated shadows stretched all the way up to the back steps of the house. Her mother's profile was in shadow too. The little girl watched her for a few seconds, then stepped into the room.

"Mother—" she said, barely croaking out the word. Her throat had suddenly gone dry.

Glancing up and seeing the expression on her daughter's face, the mother set down the pliers she had been holding. What she saw frightened her. Despite the soft rose of twilight, the little girl's complexion looked unnaturally gray. She was standing stiffly just inside the doorway as if afraid to come in farther, her arms twined awkwardly in front of her, her fingers interlocked and shoulders hunched forward. The mother rose from her chair.

"What's the matter, sweetie?" she said.

But seeing her mother move toward her, the child took a step backward and looked away. The mother hesitated.

"What is it?" she said again. Her impulse was to rush over and embrace her daughter, but she stopped herself. The child had a strange notion of dignity. She was prickly, especially if anyone appeared to feel sorry for her or concerned about her. She didn't like being helped.

"I have to tell you something," the little girl said. Her voice trembled and tears welled up in her eyes.

The mother took a silent breath to hide the apprehension that had instantly called up dreadful pictures of serious illness or injury, or some unspeakable occurrence that had done her daughter irreparable psychic damage. She stood suspended in motion before the trembling girl, afraid of scaring her away as if the child were a rabbit pausing in mid-flight. She waited and wondered.

Her daughter appeared to be trying to get control of herself. Pressing her lips together, she jutted out her chin, blinked the tears from her eyes, and swallowed. After what seemed minutes, she finally spoke, rushing her words together so hastily and in a voice so muffled by her attempts not to break down, that the mother understood nothing of what she said.

"What? Say it again, sweetie? I didn't understand you."

Having blurted it out once, the child seemed to find the courage to repeat it with more force.

"I *said*, I swallowed a button and I stole a dime and I told Meggie Edgington you liked the smell of skunks." Her face turned bright red and she burst into sobs.

Her mother didn't dare move, or breathe, or even allow an expression to settle on her face until she could fathom the significance of the child's outburst. Finally, with great delicacy, she said, "Well, Lottie, this must have worried you very much."

The little girl blinked up through her tears, searching her mother's eyes for a reaction. The mother smiled carefully; she hoped the smile would not be taken for amusement.

"When did it all happen?" she asked. And with some concern— remembering the first part of the confession but not wanting to increase her daughter's anxiety—she asked gently, "When did you swallow the button?"

"Last Christmas," the little girl sobbed out.

"Ah," said the mother, moving closer. "Quite a long time ago then."

Her daughter nodded. Between small gasps she said, "Will I have to get my stomach pumped?"

The mother could no longer restrain herself from touching her child. She walked over, leaned down and put an arm around the stooped little shoulders. The girl allowed herself to be embraced. The mother then took her by the hand and led her to the chair, where she sat down and pulled her daughter close until she stood between her knees.

Holding both her hands, the mother said, "Honey, that button went right through you a long time ago. It's not like the other time."

Not like the time three years earlier—the mother thought—when the little girl, only four years old, had swallowed the entire contents of a bottle of prescription cough medicine. The mother would never forget the terrifying events that followed the discovery of the empty bottle. For a while they couldn't find Lottie. Her husband had made a quick search of the house, then raced out to the back yard, carrying their son—two years old then—in his arms. He ran frantically from playhouse to garden to garage, shouting their daughter's name, while the mother, sick with influenza and a fever, sprang from her bed and searched the house up and down until she finally found the little girl, groggy-eyed in a cupboard that she liked to play in.

The father handed off the baby to the mother, who had gotten her daughter wrapped in a blanket. He raced to the car with the little girl over his shoulder and sped away to the hospital. In a hurried consultation, the parents had decided there was not enough time for the mother to get dressed, and it might be frightening for the two-year-old brother to witness events in an emergency room. So the mother had stayed home. It was a decision that she had regretted from that day to this.

As soon as the child was set on the examining table in that white and stainless steel emergency room she had begun screaming for her mother. Her father was helpless to soothe her. Her frantic screaming made it impossible to administer an emetic, and with time passing, it was decided lavage was called for. A tactless intern told the father in front of the child, "We'll have to pump her stomach." The father had been required then to stand back while she was strapped down and the tube put in her throat.

In bed that night, too affected by the experience to keep his feelings to himself, he had described the events in detail to his wife, tears streaming down his face. It was easy enough for her to imagine the scene; when her husband had brought the little girl back from the hospital a long two hours later, her daughter had violently wrenched herself from her father's arms and thrown herself, screaming, into her mother's.

She would never forgive herself for being careless about the cough syrup. Lottie had taken cough medicine before and knew how sweet it tasted. What had she been thinking of, not to have set the bottle on the highest shelf in a locked cupboard? She had left it on the kitchen counter, and the four-year-old had climbed up on a chair and somehow figured out the childproof cap. She was so smart, and she had a sweet tooth.

Her husband, when he'd gotten over the emergency room experience, said, "Just forget about it. Accidents happen," and she had hoped her daughter had forgotten it herself. But she often wondered whether it was after that incident that the little girl's prickliness had begun.

"They won't have to pump my stomach?" the child said.

"No honey, absolutely not."

The little girl's sobs had stopped, but she stood there mute and rigid between her mother's knees, waiting. The mother remembered there was more. Tentatively she asked, "And the dime? How did you happen to steal a dime?"

The child cast her eyes downward and held her lower lip between her teeth for a moment before mumbling, "It fell out of Christy's pocket when she was swinging by her knees, and I picked it up."

"How long ago was that?"

"In kindergarten."

The mother fought to keep tears out of her own eyes. "That's a very long time to be worried about it." Letting go of the child's hands to stroke her arms, she said, "Do you know why you picked it up?"

"I just wanted to."

"Had you already spent your allowance?"

"I didn't get an allowance then."

"Oh. That's right." A needle of guilt pricked her. "Well, Lottie, sometimes when we're little, we're not as able to resist these temptations as when we're older. I'm sure now that you're almost eight you won't do it again, will you?" The child shook her head, without speaking.

"Do you feel better now?" But she didn't seem to. Her coloring had gone from pale to red and was now back to pale again, her expression as grim as ever. The mother wondered if viewing oneself as a thief for three years would be impossible for a child to erase with a single confession. She was appalled at herself for failing to see how a five-year-old in school might need an allowance, even if only a very small one, to keep from feeling deprived and tempted. She wondered if she had any maternal intuition at all.

For a moment her face mirrored the bleakness on her daughter's face, but she quickly rallied, not wanting to inflict her mood on the already unhappy child. Smiling, she said, "Okay? All better?"

The child looked down at her hands again. She seemed as unrelieved as if no confession had been made.

"I told Meggie Edgington you liked the smell of skunks," she murmured.

A laugh rose up in the mother's throat. She bit and compressed her lips to stifle it. Taking another deep breath, she said, "Well ... I *do* like the smell of skunks."

Her daughter looked her in the eye, finally, with an expression of surprise.

"I thought ... skunks don't smell nice," she said.

"Not to most people, I guess."

"I thought it was confidential."

"Confidential?"

"Not to talk about it outside the family."

And then the mother understood. She pictured her husband at dinner, discussing finances or work problems, often afterwards leaning toward the children and leveling them with a solemn look. "I don't want this discussion to go farther than this table," he would say, and sometimes add, for emphasis: "This is *confidential*."

The mother winked at her daughter. "Well, Lottie, as far as *I'm* concerned," she said, "it's *not* confidential. I'm not ashamed of it if you aren't." She smiled, picking up the little girl's hand and patting it. "All right?"

The child nodded and allowed a tentative smile to creep onto her face. She stood for a moment more between her mother's knees, weaving her finger in and out of one of her own braids, as color returned to her face. Then she extricated herself and skipped into the next room, flipping on the light switch as she went out. In a few minutes she was curled up on the sofa completely absorbed in her book.

Chinese Puzzle

OKAY. SO HERE'S why I'm upset. I've been shunned from the Mennonite second-hand clothing store on Tenth Avenue. No, wait, that's the Amish who shun. Anyway, I've been banned. No, I'm all right. Can I take a Kleenex? Thanks. No, I'm fine.

You know The Treasure Trunk, right? You haven't been there? I got this dress there. That should give you an idea. Two dollars. Twenty-five cents for the scarf, I'm not joking. And of course the Mennonites are *committed* people. Conscientious objectors in the Vietnam War. They have convictions. They stand up for them. When they retire, they don't just say, Oh, hallelujah, let's move to Arizona and play golf eight hours a day. No. They immediately go to work at thrift stores. And even though they don't always know how to operate the most current cash register technology, they give it their best effort! Good people.

You know, sometimes you have to stand in line for fifteen, twenty minutes behind another customer at The Treasure Trunk because the volunteers are *helping* each other with the cash register. One punches the buttons, the other suggests which buttons to push— but *tactfully*, not taking over the job—and another one will be calling out the prices and snipping off the tags to take the pressure off the first two. *And* they take time to chat with the customer about the quality of the items they're purchasing. So, do you see the point I'm making? They *take time*, they work for the *poor*, and for *recycling* because Mennonites are good people. Which is why it is *so* upsetting to be banned from their store. Not banned exactly, but … knowing I can never go back. I'll have to go all the way down to the other Mennonite store on Myrtle Avenue.

Oh, what am I thinking? I can't go there *either*! Because … don't they rotate volunteers between those stores? I'm trying to remember. None The Worse For Wear is completely out of my way. I hardly ever go there. But, no, I think I can't go back to *any* Mennonite store, *period*. Unless I move out of the city.

Oh, I know I'm probably making too much of what happened. But the thing is, it's not just this one incident. It's been *building*.

I've had a guilt complex ever since the first time I went into The Treasure Trunk. I went there for a few minutes to kill time waiting for my physical therapy appointment. And the first thing I see after I walk past that section where they have all those gifts made by cooperatives of poor people in countries ruled by dictators, is these amazing dresses. The tapered bodice, the flared skirt? Like a poodle skirt without the poodle? June Cleaver dresses. You know the sitcom "Leave It To Beaver?" From the 1950s? Yes, that's the one. They have old reruns just about every week on Channel 60, 70, whatever it is.

No, now, people make fun of June Cleaver, but it's because she wore the dresses doing *housework*. *If* she hadn't carried it to that extreme, I think we would have realized that the June Cleaver look was a classic.

Anyway, on any given day, on a rack of, say, thirty dresses at The Treasure Trunk, *five or six* of them are June Cleaver dresses, and *three or four of those* are in *my size*! You *cannot find* these dresses anywhere else! Everything today is baggy, droopy, one-size-fits-all. *Or* pasted on you like glue. These June Cleaver dresses are worth their weight in *gold*, and at the Mennonite store they're cheaper than socks. And every time you go in there, there are new ones to replace the ones you've bought. I usually buy two or three. Sometimes more … but you have to understand I have been looking for these dresses since the late '80s.

I have a theory about why there are so many June Cleaver dresses at The Treasure Trunk. *Not* at the Salvation Army. *Not* the Goodwill. *Never* at the consignment shops. I noticed that a lot of these dresses are homemade. And … it's common knowledge that Mennonites sew. And the June Cleaver dresses that *aren't* homemade, have strange tags, like they come from Mennonite outlet stores or Mennonite catalogs. Now in many ways Mennonites are very *un*conventional—conscientious objection, things like that—but in *other* ways they're quite conservative—men's and women's roles and whatnot. So, here's my theory: I think *they* think women should look feminine—*waist*lines, *hips, the whole ball of wax*—but *tasteful* and feminine, not provocative, right? So, the June Cleaver dress.

Just wait, I'm getting to it. So, after several weeks of going in before my physical therapy appointments and buying dresses, one day I run in there and I grab, I don't know, maybe three … four … possibly five dresses off the rack, and I run back to the cubicle to try them on—in a hurry—because my appointment is in ten minutes and if I want to buy any of these dresses I'm going to have to stand in that interminable line at the cash register, so I am by no means *lollygagging*, you get my point? And I'm in the dressing room in my underwear, pulling the third dress over my head when this officious voice … just outside the door … calls … *loudly*, "We only have *one* dressing room and customers are *waiting*."

I have to say it irritated me. I was tempted to open the door in my underwear with the dress over my head and say, "Oh, I'm so sorry, I'll be finished in a minute." But I didn't. I did feel smug, though, when I came out ready to *buy* four dresses. But that didn't seem to make them grateful or even contrite. And then I had to wait in that long cash register bottleneck, which got even longer when I had to run and put back the fifth dress because I'd forgotten the sign in the dressing room that says, "Be Considerate Of Others. Return Clothes To Rack After Trying Them On." *And* I was late for physical therapy.

Now, I understand that with the Mennonites it isn't only about selling. A lot of it's about sharing. I *admire* that. And that's why I really didn't take offense. I didn't. I would like to mention, though, that the Mennonites moved into a bigger store sometime after that incident. I'm not saying the two situations are related. But, now they have *three* dressing rooms. That old Mennonite store was very modest in size. That's *why* it was called The Treasure *Trunk. Now*, there's a lot more space, but the prices, it seems to me, are higher. I'm not criticizing. They needed more space—obviously.

Anyway, I went into the new store, and I found some nice items— dresses—some other things—a *few* too many to carry back to the bus stop. As you know, I have back trouble. So, before checking out, I asked if I could use their phone to call a cab—I'd forgotten my cell—, and, oh my word you would have thought I was proposing a hostile takeover. "Oh, no, our telephone is for business only. We don't allow customers to use the telephone." I said, "I just need to call a taxi so I can go *home*. I don't have a car. I don't *own* a car." Which is true. I assumed they would appreciate that. Global warming and so forth.

There are *three* volunteers at the cash register, and they're look- ing at each other: what should we do, how do we handle this ex- tremely controversial situation we've never had to face before, oh dear, it's against the rules. And finally, one of them says, *sighing*, "Well, we'll have to talk with the manager." And she leaves her post and walks all the way across the store and disappears down a hallway and is gone for something like ten minutes. When she finally comes back, she says "Use line two. And limit your call to one minute." Then the three of them hover near the telephone, watching me dial so if I punch in too many numbers they'll know I'm making a long distance call.

Anyway, all of this is to give you an idea of the somewhat critical attitude I was picking up on there, although it could have been my imagination, because I know those Mennonite volunteers are good people.

So then this afternoon ... No, I'm fine. Thanks.

You have to understand the situation. And I'm not justifying myself, but I want you to know that ordinarily I wouldn't do something like this.

I went to The Treasure Trunk about forty-five minutes before my physical therapy appointment. I caught the earlier bus so I'd have time to look over the winter coats they have out. *Tell* me August is not the best season for trying on coats! The Treasure Trunk has something like one window air conditioner for about *ten thousand* square feet. But I was desperate to get a down-filled coat before they all got taken. Down is the only thing that's warm enough to keep you from freezing in this horrendous climate. Do you remember that January when we had three days at *thirty below zero*? The last water molecules still existing in the air *crystallized*! The air actually *twinkled*!

I'm not so young I can trot around in weather like that in a drafty wool jacket. I need something *enveloping*. A coat that feels like a big comforter. And to find something like that, not only warm but also good *looking*, and *cheap*, it's ... next to impossible. So anyway, I go into The Treasure Trunk and the first thing I see, right by the door on the rack of clothes they've just priced and put out, is *the* down coat.

Magnificent! Not only like new, but *mid-thigh-length*! Do you know how hard that is to find in a down coat? They're all either ankle length, so your skirt gets hiked up and bunched into a big ball between your knees when you walk, or they're cropped at the waist so your backside freezes, and of course when your backside freezes, the rest of you isn't going to be far behind, pardon the pun.

It was a gorgeous lime green color, one hundred percent cotton on the outside, no stains anywhere, double-sided zipper so you can open it at the bottom when you sit down, fully-padded detachable hood. And *pockets!* Oh, you would not have believed the *pockets!*

Anyway, I grabbed that coat off the rack, *scared to death* someone else was going to see it right at the same moment and snatch it from under my nose. Are you ready for the price? *Fifteen dollars!* And that's actually *high* for The Treasure Trunk.

I checked the label. Get this. *The label was entirely in Chinese.* Even the size was not American—40 or something like that. Chinese! This of course explains the workmanship. No, no, you're right, it's all crap *now*. But these are used clothes. They've been in closets for ages. It's *my* theory that the Chinese used to be the *only* ones who knew how to make elegantly simple, practical clothes. Do you remember in the late '80s those young women students from mainland China walking around on the university campus—*they all wore June Cleaver dresses*. And think about those China shoes. Cotton and rubber. That's it. None of your Nubuc, nylon mesh, enhanced gel cushioning blah blah blah. Cotton and rubber. I have worn this same pair of China shoes since 1990, and I bought them *second hand*. So, this is what I'm talking about. The simple, practical design strategy of the Chinese *before* the economic reforms.

Anyway, I took the coat to a dressing room. Now, the one problem that I did foresee was that it would be too big for me. Down coats always *look* big, of course, because they're filled with down. But I was afraid this one was going to be just *too* big. And, sure enough, it was huge. But—and this was my downfall—pun again, sorry—I just couldn't believe this coat wasn't going to be the one. I kept turning around, looking at it, zipping it, unzipping it. I went *outside* the dressing room and looked at it in the three-way mirrors—but there was no getting around it, it looked enormous. So I went back in the dressing room, *very* depressed. And I took it off. But as I was hanging it up, I noticed it had these massive, built-in shoulder pads.

I cannot tell you how much this annoys me. Even the *Chinese* succumbed to that god awful fad, which, although it's over now, still shows up all the time in thrift stores just to infuriate you. These huge pads that make women look like astronauts with no necks. And why in the world would anyone put them in a *down coat*!? But it occurred to me that maybe these monstrous shoulder pads were giving the coat the *illusion* of being too big. So I took a look at the inside of the coat.

The shoulder pads were built-in under the lining, not Velcroed like they sometimes are on dresses. But as I'm examining the lining of the coat, I see a pocket inside, with a long diagonal zipper. So I open this zipper pocket to check it out, as I always do when I try on clothes—because you know, people leave interesting things in the pockets, not just Kleenex. Sometimes money. It's unfortunately true nobody cleans their clothes before donating them. You'd like to believe they do. They don't.

Anyway, I unzip this pocket and I reach inside. My hand goes down into the lining all the way to the hem. And I'm thinking, what in the world would be the use of such a deep, deep pocket, and suddenly I realize this *isn't* a pocket. This is a way to get at … a second … inner … lining … that covers the down. Are you getting this picture? Two linings—one a shell for the coat, the other a shell for the down. And inside there's still another zipper that attaches this inner lining to the coat's shell. So—voilá—you can take the down lining out in order to wash the coat.

See? This was the Chinese practical way of thinking. You *have* to admire it.

So then it occurs to me that now I can easily reach inside the lining and pull out those shoulder pads.

Well, it's getting hot in this cubicle. They built three dressing rooms in an area suitable for two. Saving space. I don't blame them. But, with the minimal air conditioning, and being cooped up in such a small area with this coat, the sweat is pouring off me. But I have to find out if the coat is going to fit or not. So I reach in and unzip the lining up to the shoulder, and feel around until I find the first shoulder pad, and sure enough, I can just yank it out. The threads break, just like that. And I *don't* feel bad about doing *that*. A coat is better off without pads.

So then I dig around for the other shoulder pad, trying not to sweat all over the linings. I find it, I yank on it, but *this* one won't come loose.

Now I can hear people in the dressing rooms on either side of me, and I start to worry that pretty soon a Mennonite retiree is going to stand outside the door and shout at me. But this shoulder pad is so *stubborn*. And it's very far in where I can't see it, so I stick my *head* inside to see what I'm doing—and in this lime green sort of underwater nylon light I can just make out that the second shoulder pad is attached by heavy silk thread. Very strong! I don't know why the *other* pad came off so easily. I pull and yank. The thread slices the end of my thumb and draws blood. Can you get tetanus from thread? No, I don't think so.

Anyway, I'm sucking on my thumb to keep from dripping blood all over the fabric, and my hair is plastered to my face with sweat. And *at last* the thread breaks, and I pull the second shoulder pad out of the lining.

I had to stop to breathe. There's about fifteen minutes to go before my physical therapy appointment. I push the lining back into the coat, put the coat on and press against the wall to take a look in the mirror.

Even with the shoulder pads out, the coat is still two sizes too big for me. I am *so* sad.

I put it back on the hanger, and I'm about to return it to the rack, when I have one more idea: even if I can't wear the coat itself, the down lining alone would be well worth the fifteen dollars. I could wear it under my wool coat and then I'd be *really* warm.

So I begin to unzip the inside lining again, all the way around this time. And it's very hard to keep the outer lining from getting caught in the zipper. I can't really see what I'm doing, you know, I'm trying to tug the inside lining up through the outer lining and out through the zipper pocket. If you can picture pulling old bat insulation through the trap door of an attic crawl space? In *summer*?

Finally I get the whole thing unzipped. The padding comes loose, and I pull it free.

I stood there for a minute. Mopped my face with a shoulder pad. All of a sudden it was very quiet. Have you noticed how much noise nylon makes? It was still practically ringing in my ears. Then I hear the other people start to move around in their dressing rooms again, and I wonder if they've been pressing their ears to the wall trying to figure out what's going on. And whether there are any volunteers out there getting ready to raid the cubicle.

I have only five minutes left, so I pull the down lining on over my sweating arms and … well … the thing was gargantuan. It wasn't going to fit under my wool coat or any other coat I had.

I was … desolate.

But there was no time for grieving. In five minutes I had to put the coat back together, put it back on the rack, and run down the street to my physical therapist's office.

So I take off the down lining, pick up the coat and the outer lining which had fallen in this limp little puddle on the floor. I'll tell you, there isn't much to a down coat once the down has been removed—it's like an angora cat after a bath.

It was hard to tell which part was top, which was bottom, which was inside, which outside. And that giant zipper pocket had just vanished.

This is the kind of emergency where you have to stop and calm yourself. Close your eyes. Say an affirmation. Which I did, and when I opened my eyes I found the zipper pocket. Frantically, I stuff the padding back into the coat. But then I realize I have no idea how to match up the inner lining with the shell. That part on the *Stanford-Binet* where you have to imitate something with blocks? That's the part that brought my score down. I am not spatially gifted.

I try to push the lining sleeves back into the coat sleeves. But they're sticking to my sweaty arm. I'm *trying* not to rustle the nylon, but *you* try not rustling nylon. The sound is deafening. I'm sure the Mennonites are standing outside that door on the verge of calling Mennonite security. *And* I can't find the end of the wretched zipper! I'm probing, prodding, digging all the way down as far as I can go. And then, all of a sudden, there it is. I have the padding's zipper tab in one hand and the end of the shell's zipper in the other, I fit them together and pull up.

And they fall apart. Pull up. Fall apart.

Twenty times, thirty, I don't know, time is stretching out. My life is passing before me. And no matter what I do, these *worthless, Satanic, Communist zipper teeth will not mesh*, even though they were meshed *before*—obviously—they *had* to be.

That's when I began to wonder if things I'd believed for years were untrue. That the Chinese had *not* been practical. The Mennonites were *not* good people. That it didn't matter, it just didn't matter if I left the whole shriveled mess hanging *limp* off that one—completely inadequate—little hook they provide you with or if I just dumped it on the floor.

The big problem now was not whether it was *wrong* to leave this disemboweled garment for *them* to figure out how to put back together, or whether I should carry the thing over to the counter and lay down fifteen bucks for *nothing*. The big problem now was how I could leave that pathetic wreck of a coat in the dressing room and get out of there without anybody seeing me.

It was wrong, I know. I've never done anything like it before. But think of Jean Valjean, for example—did you see *Les Miz*?—Well, should *he* have been condemned for stealing that loaf of bread? Of course it was stealing, but still!

I had no idea who or what I'd see when I came out. I listened and cracked the door open.

The dressing room area was, amazingly, deserted.

As nonchalantly as I could, I glided across the floor past the cash registers. All three volunteers were busy with a customer, and I got as far as the exit. Then, just as I was sidling out the door, one of the volunteers looked up. And this is what's been *gnawing* at me: *I don't know if she saw my face and will connect it later with that thing in the dressing room.*

Without knowing that, how can I risk going back there?

Thanks. I knew you'd sympathize.

So—and this is one reason I called you to come over. On my way past the cash register, as I was going by the dress rack, there was a—what would you call the color? Chartreuse?—dress. Fitted bodice, flared skirt. I only saw it out of the corner of my eye. But I was wondering ... do you have like just fifteen minutes—*ten* minutes—to drive over there before the store closes and check the size? I can wear either a 12 or a 14—depends on the cut. And if you happen to notice any others like it ... ? Oh, you're a *doll*. Thank you so much.

A Little Something for Everyone

AT EVERY CORNER the same sign has appeared, decorated with hand-drawn picnic baskets draped with red and white gingham napkins:

Jenners' Neighborhood Annual Cook-out!
Sunday, August 18th, 5:00 – 8:00 PM at Maple Court Park.
Peg and Joe will provide their famous smoked meats to grill
as usual. BYO side dish, drinks, plates and utensils.
Dress kids for getting wet. Splash pad open all evening.
SEE YOU THERE!

He thinks, well, that'll be a good way to meet more of the neighbors. The kids will like it.

So far since they moved in, the people next door on both sides and across the street have been friendly. If anything, they've been hyper-friendly, but that's better than the alternative.

The small, one-block-square park is three streets from their house. They haul their towels and picnic basket in their son's wagon. Seven years old, but he still likes to pull it. The little girl clamors for a ride. Their mother takes out the basket, and the boy helps his sister to climb in, clutching the small teddy bear she has named Bobo. The boy's skinny arms strain as he pulls the laden wagon uphill. His mother says, "That weighs too much for you, honey" and starts to lift their daughter out.

"No it doesn't," their son protests.

"Let him pull her," he says. The boy likes to carry his sister in the wagon to prove how strong he is. "It's not that far."

He and his wife hold hands as they walk the distance to the park. They've come a little late, and everything is already in full swing. His wife sets the basket down on a narrow open space at one of the extra picnic tables the city has brought in. The people sitting at the table obligingly move over to make more room. They all exchange greetings and introductions.

There are two smoking grills in the park. A man and woman poke the coals with long-handled spatulas. They wear white butcher's aprons with logos: "MEAT AND POTATOES GUY" and "I'M WITH MEAT AND POTATOES GUY." A large cooler for the meat sits on the ground next to each of them.

His sociable son heads for the splash pad and joins the frolicking, shrieking kids running in and out of the fountains. His wife takes the little girl by the hand and they stand with other parents encouraging nervous younger children and babies to dip an arm or a leg into the spray. His daughter isn't sure about getting wet. She wants to go on the swings instead. He comes over, takes her by the hand and sets her gently in one of the baby swings. She's already almost three, and it's just barely big enough for her.

"Push, Daddy!" she shouts.

He stands behind her and pushes, enjoying the solid impact of his palm on her soft, sturdy little back, and soon he's lost in the rhythmic, repetitive arc of her body through the air. It reminds him of the pendulum on his parents' beloved grandfather clock. The clock hypnotized him when he was a child. He would watch it for fifteen minutes at a time, waiting for the resonant bong bong bong to sound. His daughter is silent and solemn, completely in the moment. She's a quiet child, an introvert. So is he—most comfortable with family, a few friends, not too much commotion.

The evening is warm but without oppressive humidity. The air feels soft on his bare forearms. From his post behind his daughter he surveys the scene: the swings for toddlers and older kids; the jungle gym and slide where parents hover close to keep the little ones from going too fast; the smoking grills and their jolly attendants; the picnic tables under the shade of thick maples where parents sit leaning backwards, chatting and looking on; a couple of benches occupied by elderly folks. At a distant corner of the park the low, heavy branch of a massive larch tree provides a perch from which a trio of teenage girls swing their feet at the teasing boys below. And now some kids, eleven or twelve years old, kick a soccer ball into the street, which the city has blocked off with traffic cones.

It's all contained in this postage stamp-sized neighborhood park. A little something for everyone, he thinks. Somehow it reminds him of that Dutch artist's scene of peasants taking their leisure at the end of the day. Pastoral.

The meat is grilled. People line up, are served and sit at the tables to eat. They hoist paper cup toasts to the chefs. After dinner, the kids race back to their play as if to beat the oncoming night and the end of festivities.

Now the sun has sunk low behind the old maples. Families, a few at a time, are beginning to gather up belongings and head home. The chefs' grandson carries a bucket of water from the tap at the drinking fountain to douse the coals. The teenage girls and boys have abandoned the tree and sauntered off in a clump, seeking entertainments away from the eyes of their parents.

He calls to his son that they'll be going home soon, but the boy is having too much fun playing two-man soccer with his new friend and pretends not to hear. Their daughter has become sleepy-eyed, and his wife lays her down on a dry towel on the grass.

A few fireflies blink on and off.

He and his wife have no objection to lingering. They sit shoulder to shoulder at the picnic table and talk about nothing important, just the day and the things that need to be done tomorrow to finish getting moved in before their jobs start. They could talk about how they stick out here, but that's such a given it's not worth mentioning.

Finally, their son's friend goes home with his parents, and they load the picnic basket and wet towels into the wagon.

By now it's almost dark and, without their noticing when it began, the night pulses with the rasp of cicadas.

They take the walk back slowly, enjoying the cool night air. He carries his daughter, who is asleep against his shoulder. His wife puts her arm around his waist. Their son runs downhill pulling the wagon.

At the end of the first block, his daughter stirs and looks around with the unfocused gaze of the newly wakened. Then her body tenses with alarm.

"My Bobo!" she shrieks, twisting in his arms. "Where is my Bobo?"

They check the wagon. The bear is not there.

"She must have dropped it somewhere," his wife says, unfazed by the tragic crumpling of their daughter's face and the impending howl of lamentation.

"I'll run back and find it," he says, transferring his crying daughter to his wife's arms. "Go on. I'll catch up with you." He doesn't like to leave them walking alone at this time of night and takes off running.

But it's also exhilarating to sprint up the hill after all the sitting and standing he's done this evening. At the park he quickly checks on top of and underneath the picnic tables, doesn't find the bear and looks off toward the swings. It's lying, a small dark form, on the ground. He trots over, grabs it, and takes off again. Picking up his pace, he races across the park to the sidewalk.

His heart lurches at the deafening shriek of a siren behind him. Just as suddenly, the sound dies away. Then he hears the clunk of car doors opening by the curb. He turns. The squad car is angled so the headlights shine on him. His heart starts to beat very fast.

"Drop it and put your hands in the air!" Two cops are getting out, guns drawn.

For a split second, he doesn't know what he's supposed to drop. And then he does. He throws it down. It lands in the dark grass by the sidewalk.

"Keep your hands in the air and walk slowly over here. Slowly. Keep 'em high."

Almost foolishly, one foot at a time in slow motion, he makes his way to the squad car. Together the two cops shove him hard against the door.

They could kill him in an instant. The neighborhood is dark. There's no one to see.

"What are you doing here?" the one cop asks.

He won't be able to stand it if they hear his voice gone weak. His jaw is trembling so hard his teeth are rattling.

"Answer when you're asked a question! Are you resisting arrest?"

He takes a deep breath before speaking. His voice cracks.

"I live here," he says.

"Oh yeah?" One cop holds the point of the gun against his back while the other pats him down and pulls his wallet from his pocket.

The cop shuffles through the contents and takes out his driver's license. He examines it with a small flashlight, turns him around and squints back and forth several times from the photo to his face. He reads the address aloud.

"You say you live here?" he says. "You want to explain this address? In *Columbus*, Ohio? Is this *your* wallet?"

"We just moved here from there."

"Uh huh. Convenient."

With a sudden clarity shining through the fog of his fear, he remembers his new faculty ID, just issued that week. "If you keep looking, you'll find my University photo ID," he says. But it occurs to him that this may be pointless. The photos on the ID and the license are of no use to the cop because … *He can't tell if I look like the pictures.*

The cop puts a little distance between them, points the gun at his chest. To his partner he says, "Get that thing out of the grass." The partner strides to the lawn and picks it up. He holds it to the glare of the headlights.

"Jesus," he calls back. "It's a fucking teddy bear."

"Oh Christ," says the other cop. He lowers his gun. The two men shake their heads ruefully, exchanging wry smiles. The bear is a joke on themselves.

The cops put their guns away. He is given back his wallet. The bear is tossed out of his reach, and he has to bend down to pick it up off the pavement.

Then one of the cops tilts his head and narrows his eyes, thinking.

"What are you doing with that toy?" he says. "In the park?"

The full force of the implication hits him in the chest. He can hardly breathe.

"There was a picnic," he says. His voice is high and shaky.

"A picnic," says the other cop. "At this time of night."

"A neighborhood picnic. Earlier. I have a two-year-old. She left the bear behind." He fumbles in the wallet and manages to pull out a photo of his family.

"And why exactly were you running?"

Why was he running? Because … running felt good … and because his family was vulnerable on a dark street.

"My wife and kids were waiting for me."

The cops look at each other. In that look they seem to come to a decision.

"Well, we got a call reporting someone suspicious running across the park."

"We had to check it out," the other cop adds. They move toward the car.

The cop gets into the driver's seat and the other one goes around to the passenger side.

The driver rolls down his window part way and says, not looking at him, "It was just a misunderstanding."

He pulls out onto the street, makes a U turn and, drives away.

Walking slowly, he catches up to his family halfway down the block to their house.

His daughter sees the bear dangling by its legs in his hand.

"Bobo!" she cries, joyously.

He thrusts the bear into her outstretched arms.

"Here," he says. "Don't kill anyone with it."

His wife stares at him.

"Where … was it?" she says.

"Where do you think it was? In the park."

They walk the rest of the way home without speaking.

The Handkerchief

I N CLASS THAT afternoon I failed to notice Roger's predicament at first because I was daydreaming that I was a plain but oddly attractive governess in an English manor house where the lord of the manor was laying siege to my righteous principles.

An intricate perspective drawing of the mansion's rooms and gardens decorated the margins of the vocabulary list I was supposed to be studying. In case Mr. Halsey should notice my regular lifting and replacing the paper as I applied my pen, I kept the drawing hidden under a folded sheet of paper that I used as a blind for testing myself on vocabulary definitions. But the teacher was not likely to suspect me; I was a model student.

Roger Nyles was not. His blank eyes and half-open mouth gave away the chronic state of boredom, frustration, and confusion of the slow learner. The teacher wouldn't help him, and our classmates didn't dare to. Roger himself had apparently learned to keep quiet rather than make himself conspicuous by asking obvious questions.

I felt benevolent toward Roger because he had once said hello to me in the hall as I was leaving school to go home. He had no reason to say hello; students were surging by, stopping to tie their shoelaces or arrange their stacks of books, but he had stood just inside the door as I passed and said hello, his ears turning red. I wasn't particularly flattered. He was poor and shabby and shy and

I felt sorry for him. But I understood that he liked me, and so I felt a magnanimous warmth.

I hadn't noticed that he was suffering that afternoon when I looked up from my notebook, but saw that, unaccountably, he was the focus of the teacher's anger. Mr. Halsey had stood up and was staring at him sardonically.

The room became very quiet. Just the radiators, pinging and clanking and spitting like cats, broke the long silence. Captured on three sides by my old-fashioned school desk, I looked out the steamy window. Beyond the playing fields were snow-covered houses, a bootless woman picking her way along the un-shoveled sidewalk, gray clouds in a low sky. I watched them and hated the terrible, familiar thing that I knew was about to happen. I despised the squirmy, guilty relief I felt, knowing that I was exempt, that by being well-dressed and clever and ingratiating, I would always avoid the humiliating plight that was about to descend on Roger Nyles.

Roger was still looking startled even after enduring thirty seconds or more of Mr. Halsey's satirical gaze. He had no idea why he was suddenly being singled out.

On a deep inhalation, Mr. Halsey caused the mucous in his nose to rattle, loud and long. I sensed that this was a repetition; while I had been daydreaming, the teacher had been pointedly staring at Roger while sniffing and, again, sniffing.

Roger's eyes were wary. He looked at the teacher, looked away, looked back again and then stubbornly returned the stare, his cheeks and lips quivering. In my own cheeks and lips I felt what it was for him to keep his heart from showing through his face.

Finally, Mr. Halsey spoke.

"Am I to assume that you don't carry a handkerchief, Mr. Nyles?"

Roger's eyes narrowed.

"Whaddaya mean?" he said in a cracking voice, and blushed.

"Whaddaya mean!" imitated Mr. Halsey. "Whaddaya mean!" The teacher smiled and raised his thick red eyebrows in mock surprise. "Mr. Nyles doesn't know what I mean! I could swear I was speaking English, or at least I started out my sentence in English. Did it suddenly turn into Swahili?"

The class tittered dutifully.

"Let me say it louder in case your head is so full of phlegm that your ears have become stopped up. Am I to assume that you do not carry a handkerchief?"

The radiator hissed and rattled.

"I dunno," Roger said, at last.

Mr. Halsey traveled swiftly down the aisle to Roger's desk in the back and stood over him, forcing him to tilt his head uncomfortably in order to return stare for stare. After a moment Roger lowered his eyes and focused on the seatback in front of him. The teacher sniffed again. He sniffed four times, wrinkling his nose, exaggerating, putting his shoulders into the performance.

"Do you know how hard it is for your classmates to study when they have to listen to your sniff, sniff, sniffling all afternoon?"

Roger's lips and jaw were working. He stared straight ahead.

"Do you *own* a handkerchief?"

Roger didn't answer.

Mr. Halsey glanced up at the rest of us, a comedian about to deliver the punch line.

"Doesn't your mother know enough to give you a handkerchief and explain its use?"

A little gleam of wetness appearing in one of Roger's nostrils made me hold my breath. He was shivering in his thin, short-sleeved shirt with one button missing just above the beltline. A gap of pale skin showed. Sweat ran down my back.

Mr. Halsey drew a large, clean, white handkerchief from his jacket pocket and held it out in the air above Roger's nose.

"I am going to give you a gift, Mr. Nyles. I hope you will use it from now on."

He dropped it, and everyone watched it float and come to rest on the top of Roger's hand.

Roger let it lie there. From his nostril to the top of his upper lip, the wetness now formed a slender stream.

Mr. Halsey walked back to the front of the room and sat on his desk with his short legs dangling. He folded his hands in his lap and brought his eyebrows into an arch of world-weary patience. The minute hand on the large round clock over the door moved jerkily from 2:20 to 2:25.

At last, Mr. Halsey said pleasantly, "If you can't bring yourself to use a handkerchief, Mr. Nyles, we really don't want you in this classroom."

I forced myself to turn from the clock to Roger's eyes and dripping nose. He was still staring at the desk in front of him.

All at once he raised his hand, letting the handkerchief flutter to the floor. With a quick movement he pulled his shirttail out and swiped it across his nose. Then he stood up awkwardly, banging his hip against the back of his desk, and walked out of the room, letting the door stand open. I turned quickly to catch the teacher's expression.

Mr. Halsey was still smiling blandly. He stood up and took a thick wooden ruler from a bouquet of rulers in a ceramic pot on his desk. Then he walked casually down the aisle and, stooping only a little, scooped the handkerchief up with the end of the ruler, carried it out in front of him back up the aisle, and dropped it in the metal wastebasket.

Immediately he turned his back to the class and wrote on the board: "The Helping Verbs." He tapped the blackboard with the chalk, which splintered slightly, and the first student in the back row called out the first word. One by one, the helping verbs were listed.

After the helping verbs, he erased the board and, still with his back to the students, wrote "The Fifty-Two Prepositions." I knew all fifty-two. I had memorized them in alphabetical order to the tune of Tchaikovsky's "Waltz of the Flowers," but I didn't speak up. It took him twenty minutes to eke the information out of my classmates.

"Aboard, about, above, across, after, against, along, amid, among, around, at," I sang inside my head . . . "Before, behind, below, beneath, beside, between, beyond, but, by . . ." I stared into the teacher's back with a reserved, stony face that was meant to convey hatred so subtly that if he turned around he wouldn't be able to tell if my expression was defiant or studious. I had just won the spelling contest for the fifth week in a row. My big red Excellence Certificate lay conspicuously atop my notebook. I thrust it inside.

When Mr. Halsey did finally turn around, he shot a quick, almost imperceptible glance at the open door and then walked briskly to his desk and sat down. With a benevolent smile, he now directed the advanced learners to work on their poetry projects while he led the slow learners in a reading comprehension exercise. It took me about a minute to finish the assignment; then, circling my paper with a protective arm and pretending to be absorbed in the contemplation of metaphors, I turned my head a little sideways to sneak a look at the still open door and the six or seven feet of hallway visible beyond it.

Roger Nyles was not in sight. What I could see of the hall was an emptiness that could almost be heard and smelled: hollow, echoing, waxy, metallic. Was Roger standing alone out there in that large, quiet corridor, just out of view? Listening? Waiting? Wondering what to do next?

Where would he go? Could a thirteen-year-old boy simply leave school in the middle of the day without being sick or called home? I pictured the hawk-like swooping and pouncing such an event would set loose in my own household. What would his parents say and do? Maybe instead of going home he would go out to the playing field, wait there on a bench in the snow until school was out. I couldn't remember if he had boots. Possibly he was standing in the cloakroom among the jackets and coats doing terrible, humiliating things to Mr. Halsey in his mind, resolving never to come back.

He would be made to come back, I was sure. It was against the law not to go to school. I imagined him in the principal's office, not talking, sitting in a chair with his arms folded across his chest or hanging down at his sides. No, how was it that he characteristically sat? With one hand clasping the opposite wrist, and one foot jiggling against the leg of the chair. Yes, that was how he would be sitting as they called his parents and tried to get him to explain himself.

It occurred to me that they would call Mr. Halsey in, too. I was surprised they hadn't done so already. Maybe they wanted to wait until everyone could be there at the same time—parents, teacher, principal, guilty party—all together in one room. How would Roger be able to face Mr. Halsey again?

I looked at the teacher. He was telling the slow learners a humorous story which, from their relatively unguarded expressions, must not have been at their expense. He was being deliberately kind and helpful to the slow learners now, I thought, because this might be the moment someone from the office would poke a head in the door and ask for him. But no one came, and there were only five minutes remaining in class.

I conjectured further: Roger had run away, not from school but from Mr. Halsey, so maybe they would put him in another seventh grade English class—there were three. Would they come up with a solution that simple? But as far as I knew there wasn't any circumstance short of some tragic physical condition which would persuade school authorities to change existing arrangements just because the arrangements caused a student anguish. No, there was no doubt that they would return him to the classroom, and I thought of Roger's shame, his walking, beaten, through that door to face the teacher's unrestrained, victorious sarcasm. I couldn't stand it.

Someone must save Roger. Someone must act as a witness on his behalf. *I* could do it. I could inform on Mr. Halsey, go right to the principal's office and report what I had seen.

Poor Roger Nyles couldn't be articulate or credible, not like me, with my unmitigated record of "S's" for Superior in every single box of every grid on every grade card since kindergarten. Straight "S's" in each category from "Reading" and "Arithmetic" to "Deport-ment" and "Getting Along with Others." With superiority glowing in my veins, my blood raced and my heart pounded at the thrill of a self-imposed challenge. I hadn't been able to imagine defending my*self*, were I in Roger's place, but, not being in his place, I could easily imagine defending *him*.

Now I put myself in the hallway, walking resolutely to the office as soon as the bell would ring, not even stopping to get my coat and hat, but just going straight there, before I could change my mind. That was how I would get myself to do it. No second thoughts; I wouldn't even plan what I would say but just go and tell what hap-pened and why it was unfair.

The bell rang. I jumped up and quickly gathered my books and papers into my trembling arms. The students had to file out by rows, mine always last because of its being next to the window, and I last of all, from sitting in the front. I hugged my notebooks to my chest. What if the Principal were already walking out the door to go home? What if the trial were just now getting over, without the teacher? I pushed forward.

"Miss Bradley!" called Mr. Halsey. "I want to talk to you."

I stopped. I knew he couldn't literally read my mind, but for a moment I wondered if he had some inner eye that could spot Good and overpower it with Evil. I turned around.

"Miss Bradley, would you share your insights from your poetry project with the class tomorrow? I want you to lead the discussion, and I'll have the secretary type up your analysis and make dittoes for everyone in the class so they'll have your ideas in front of them. Your classmates seem to have a give-up attitude about poetry." Standing behind his desk, he planted his hands flat on it and leaned a little toward me as if about to let me in on a secret. "I'd like them to discover, as you have, that poetry can grip and compel the imagination."

I found Mr. Halsey's suggestion irresistibly flattering.

"All right," I said. I set my backpack on the desk and fumbled in it for my notebook. I tore out the pages of my project and handed them to him. His pale blue eyes and soft, jowly cheeks beamed across at me, level with my face. I had grown very tall in the last year and realized that Mr. Halsey in middle age was no taller than I was at thirteen. It made me take a step closer.

"Mr. Halsey," I said, breathlessly, "don't you think you should have been nicer to Roger Nyles?"

The effect of my question on his face was remarkable. The arched eyebrows curved higher while the heavy eyelids drooped lower as if—from boredom—they found small inducement for holding themselves up. A mild, close-lipped sneer appeared, giving him the look of a sleepy lizard with its eye on a blundering fly.

"'Nicer,'" he said, blandly. "'Nicer' than *what*, may I ask? When you use the comparative form, Miss Bradley, you must put it in context."

"Roger didn't do anything wrong," I blurted out. "I didn't even *notice* him sniffing." My voice was high and shaky and I was afraid I would start to cry. "He may *never* learn English *now*."

Immediately I wished I could un-say it. The hooded eyes flew open. The mild sneer turned into a terrible smile.

"That boy does not want to learn English." He enunciated each word as if I were hard of hearing. "Like most of his classmates, he does not want to learn anything unless it's pleasant. It is not, I repeat, not, a teacher's job to make things pleasant. Life is not pleasant and there are many, many unpleasant things he will have to learn to do in life whether he wants to or not. In the future, no one is going to say"—here he affected a falsetto voice—'Oh Mr. Nyles, you don't want to come to work today? That's fine. Just stay home and take a nice long nap. What? You don't wish to pay your income taxes? Well, why should you? Save your money and buy yourself a color television set.' " Now he was full into the performance, mincing back and forth behind his desk. "'You'd rather sit there and let everyone else carry the load? Why of course, Mr. Nyles. *We'll* handle it for you!' No," he continued in his own voice, "they'll kick him off the job, they'll throw him in jail, they'll shun him. Would it be 'nicer' of me to let him go along believing he can get away with these things?"

"But he doesn't get away with things," I protested. "He's just quiet and ... he didn't *have* a handkerchief."

"And he thumbs his nose at the teacher and he doesn't do his work and he runs away from his responsibilities." Mr. Halsey paused. "Do you know how many of my students have come back to thank me after they've been out in the world for a few years? They shake my hand and shake my hand again! 'Mr. Halsey,' they say, 'I hated you then, but I'm glad now that you taught me the importance of discipline. You didn't let me get away with anything. Thank you! Thank you!'"

"How many?" I asked.

"How *many*?"

"How many have come back like that?"

"Dozens!"

"They didn't care that you made fun of them?"

His upper lip curled and his eyes narrowed. "Would you like to give me a single instance of my *ever* making fun of someone?"

My mind went back to Mr. Halsey's sniffing and sniffing. It was the only thing I could think of. The other incidents had momentarily vanished. But now the sniffing seemed a rather pale illustration.

"Well?"

I was silent.

"Did I, for example, make *fun* of Mr. Nyles when I offered him my own clean handkerchief so that he could wipe his running nose, which must have been causing him a great deal of discomfort?"

I gave no answer.

"Did I make fun of him when I explained the etiquette of using a handkerchief—information that apparently no one else had ever taken the time or had the kindness to offer him?"

Silence.

"It's a great disservice to people to let them go through life ignorantly embarrassing themselves just because one is afraid of offending them. That is the height of selfishness, in my opinion."

I could not accept this. He seemed to be turning every mean thing he had said or done into an act of kindness.

"But it depends on how you say it," I protested.

He paused. I saw his cheeks twitch and forced myself to keep my eyes on his face.

"Maybe you would like to offer an illustration of 'how I say it,' since I gather you have some considerable expertise in linguistics?"

I didn't know what he was asking. I hesitated.

He smiled. "You'll learn that it's a lot easier to accuse than to provide evidence," he said.

Evidence, he wanted. Examples. A moment before, I couldn't have given even one, but now a flood of remarks and incidents poured into my mind, incidents I had recounted many times to classmates, friends, occasionally to my family, in Mr. Halsey's very own voice. I was a born mimic with an ear for intonation, inflection, affectation, timing. Mr. Halsey was easy to do. I looked him in the eye.

"'Doesn't your mother know enough to give you a handkerchief and explain its use?'" I sneered in that sarcastic tone, ending with the characteristic lift of the eyebrows and tight-lipped smile.

He grabbed my arm, then immediately dropped it. His face grew red. He turned from me and sat down at his desk.

"Did it occur to you, Miss Bradley, that *you* interpret that as making fun of somebody because you evidently enjoy ridiculing others yourself?"

My indignation soared. Never did I make fun of people! Never! This was a rule I took very seriously, never to embarrass or humiliate anyone by a personal remark, no matter how provoked. When my younger brother caught a glimpse of me in underpants for the first time since I had begun to mature, and he made fun of my broadening backside, even then I had not retaliated with a comment about his prominent ears or his small size, things I knew he was sensitive about. My imitations, yes, these were a way of making fun, but always affectionately, never in mockery, except in the absolutely rare case, as with Mr. Halsey, when the original unquestionably deserved it!

"I'm *not* ridiculing you," I said defiantly, my face hot. "That's just how you sound!"

He picked up a ruler and tapped it on his palm.

"As a matter of fact, young lady, I am not unduly repulsed *or* intimidated by ridicule. I don't consider it as cardinal a sin as you seem to, though you indulge in it hypocritically—"

"I don't—!" He waved away my interruption with a stab in the air of the ruler.

"Do you know why I am not afraid of it? Because it can be strengthening. Let me tell you something. If you make yourself immune to ridicule, you will forever be an independent person in both thought and action."

He walked around the desk and, to my surprise, took me firmly but gently by the arm and drew me over to the window. He pointed down toward the south playing field where several boys were lingering after school. They were throwing snowballs at one another, tussling, and stuffing snow down each other's jackets. Seeing them, I had the passing thought that I should leave school by the north door.

"Look at those boys down there. They don't have your sensibilities, Miss Bradley, far from it. They will mercilessly dig out each other's wistful little secrets and hidden thoughts and figuratively rub them in the snow until they are frozen or cut off from the air that gives them life. That is how they naturally treat each other. And if an odd boy comes along, whose spots of vulnerability are different from the rest, oh, then watch the fun! They'll hunt him down as if he were some kind of rare animal, like the snow leopard. Have you ever seen pictures of that beautiful creature? It's white all over under its spots. Very, very rare. Almost extinct. Because, of course, it's hunted ferociously by those who see anything unique as a target. Still, the strongest of these animals have survived." He folded his arms and turned to look at her.

"You misplace your energetic advocacy, Miss Bradley, although I admire you for it. Roger Nyles may not be the most popular boy in class, but neither is he a snow leopard. It's true, he's small and doesn't dress well, but he has the advantage of being stupid in school, which is in his favor, since there's nothing the others hate more than an intelligent boy. To be teased for being small or fat or for having a funny name, that's negligible. A boy who agonizes over such trivial things isn't worth his salt. Roger's stupidity, however, that is something else again. I have a duty to chide him about that, since no one else will."

What he said about agonizing over trivial things seemed very wrong to me. I was considering how my twelve-year-old brother suffered quietly and miserably over being one of two Richards in his class—Big Richard and, of course, Little Richard—and how, given the circumstances, he had no choice but to use the full form of his name, its formality the price he had to pay to escape the nickname Little Dick. His misery didn't seem at all trivial to me.

Mr. Halsey continued, his voice bubbling over with mirth.

"And if you take a boy who is not only small and dresses oddly and has a funny name, but also stutters, you have an irresistibly humorous situation indeed." He laughed. His laugh sounded hearty and almost genuine, like a well-executed stage laugh, but it didn't look genuine; his eyes didn't participate in it. A fine sweat glistened on his forehead. He reached in his pocket for his handkerchief, which, of course, was lying at the bottom of the wastebasket. He shook his head in its direction and ostentatiously pursed his lips as if trying to suppress a sudden hilarity.

He said, "I'll tell you a very funny story that happened to me when I was about your age. You're a smart girl, so I'm sure you'll see the point."

I looked at the clock. It was already quarter after three. I had forgotten about getting to the Principal's office. It was probably too late now. I began to feel uneasy remaining in the room with Mr. Halsey.

He said, still chuckling, "You may have guessed that I had a bit of a stammer myself as a child. Well, *quite* a stammer, as a matter of fact."

"You did?" I hadn't guessed.

"If it surprises you that's because, if nothing else, I am, as we all know, a great talker—a virtuoso, you could say." He winked at me.

"But there's a reason for that, which you'll understand in a minute." He looked out the window again. The boys were beginning to drift toward home.

"As I say, I was a stutterer. Now, you are proud of your imitations. But you know, Miss Bradley, there isn't a boy over the age of five who cannot imitate a stutterer expertly. Your Roger, I'm sure, is as good at it as the rest of them. As you can imagine, I tried my best not to give them the opportunity. Fortunately, I was very smart and I was like that snow leopard I told you about. I could blend into my surroundings. As long as I kept my mouth shut, sat at the back of the room, and took alternate routes home, I was relatively safe. But now, here's the funny part. I happened to have a terrible crush on a girl in my class. Jean, her name was. She was a lively, smart girl, not idiotic like the rest, but down-to-earth and very sweet looking, with lovely black hair and pretty pink cheeks and a warm, sincere smile. Everybody liked her. And I liked her best of all.

"She would say hello to me and occasionally ask me about a homework assignment, which may not sound like much to you, and, of course, it didn't mean anything." He laughed again. "I was intelligent enough to know that she was just being nice. Can you imagine how absurd it would have been to think that she had any special feeling for me? No, I didn't have any such thought, but I was grateful to her for asking me questions, knowing how long it always took me to get my answer out. This didn't seem to bother her!" He stopped for a moment and opened the window a crack. It was very hot in the room.

"At any rate," he continued, "I made a big mistake. The kind of mistake you make when you're that age." He winked at me again. "And let it be a lesson to you not to write anything in those note-books of yours you wouldn't want to fall into the wrong hands." I looked down at my notebook, which I was clutching to my chest, and thought of my manor houses and drawings of elegant ladies with hairdos like wedding cakes.

"I was something of a poet," he said, "and I wrote a poem about her. It didn't survive, so I can't judge now, but in looking back, I think it may actually have been a good poem, considering the age I was when I wrote it. An exceptionally sensitive poem, though probably too much on the romantic side."

I began to feel very uncomfortable. This was so close to my own life, my own secrets, and he was a middle-aged man whose private life the students knew nothing about. None of us even knew his first name because he went by his initials, R. K. In private among the students the other teachers were referred to by their first names, the sterner ones by nicknames to take the edge off their power. Mrs. Stamp was "Vickie." Mr. Carleton, the Principal, was "Freddie." But Mr. Halsey had no life that was known to us and no nickname. Once, someone suggested calling him "Hellsey," but it didn't catch on.

I wanted very much to leave now, but Mr. Halsey seemed to find it perfectly natural to be talking with me in this way, giving me this intimate glimpse into his past, and he continued his story, apparently unconcerned at how increasingly hard it was for me to look him in the eye.

"Well, there was a little band of hellions," he said, "who had been enjoying themselves at my expense ever since I entered school in the first grade." He shrugged. "They didn't really bother me. I was used to them. But, of course, they were getting older now, and were developing more imaginative ways of torturing their peers. One day, I left my notebook in the classroom during the lunch hour. To make a long story short, they found the poem I had written to Jean and made off with it.

"Well, that afternoon, innocent of what had happened, I started home from school and, just as I came around the side of the school building, three of these little bandits grabbed me from behind and hauled me off to a secluded area behind the playground where I saw Jean standing and talking to two of the others. She seemed surprised to see me, and, in that moment, as I stepped forward to say hello, the two boys grabbed her and held her arms behind her back. Now you might think the girl would be scared, but, with her trusting good nature, she just struggled a little and protested, laughing and saying they'd better let her go or else!

"Well, I still didn't know what this was about. I'd kept my love for her a deep secret. Then, with great formality, the meanest of these boys—Colin, his name was—pulled my poem from his jacket pocket. Well, I recognized it immediately.

"'Oh, Roscoe,'" he said. Here, Mr. Halsey stopped abruptly as he realized what he had revealed. Mr. Halsey's name was Roscoe! I looked at him, wide-eyed. I was the only student in the school who now knew this, and it made me fearful of the penalty it might incur; my face must have looked serious. He seemed confused for a moment, or, not confused, exactly, but surprised. Surprised at himself for having let out this secret? No, I realized he was surprised that I hadn't laughed. As if I would dare! Slowly he resumed his story.

"He said, 'Roscoe, did you *lose* something?' This boy waved my poem in my face. I was, of course, unable to say a word. Then he turned to Jean, laughing—they were all laughing, giggling like hyenas—and he said, 'Jean, Roscoe is going to read you a poem. He made it up *all* by himself, didn't you Roscoe?' And he thrust the poem under my nose and held it there. 'Go ahead and read your poem, Roscoe, but don't make any m-m-m-mistakes. If you m-m-m-make any mistakes, you'll have to s-s-s-start over until you g-g-g-get it right!'

"Well, the others thought this was great fun. Absolutely hilarious! They laughed. They clapped. 'Come on, Roscoe,' they said.

'Read your poem to your true love!' I shook my head, no, as if I actually had a choice *not* to read the thing. And then Colin said, 'Rahhh-scoe, we're going to have to keep Jean here until you do it. You don't want her mother to get worried, do you?' I heard Jean say, 'You let me go, and let him go, too. I don't want to hear a poem!' 'No, no,' they said, 'you *have* to hear Roscoe's bee*yoo*tiful, bee*yoo*tiful poem!' "

Here Mr. Halsey sat down on the desk, swinging his short legs from side to side and gripping the edge of the desktop. He smiled. I forced myself to smile back.

"Well," he said. "Here's where the fun began! You can picture just how ludicrous I must have looked! They said, 'Roscoe, start reading or we're going to pull your pants down!'" Mr. Halsey let out a peculiarly loud guffaw.

"You should have seen me! You can bet I began to read that poem as fast as I could. I concentrated as if my life depended on it!" He closed his eyes, recollecting. "Let's see, I believe I can remember a few words … uh …

'Jean, you move, as if a squirrel upon a tree,
Bright-eyed, daring, graceful, gay and free …'"

He opened his eyes. "Some such stuff as that. I really can't remember. And, oh! You can imagine they were beside themselves! 'Run up that tree, Jean. Shake your tail, Jean.' They were getting quite a lot of quotable material out of that one, I can tell you. I kept reading until, inevitably, I stumbled on a word—it was a very *long* poem." Gesturing broadly, mocking himself, Mr. Halsey recited another line.

"'And only you, of all the heedless throng,
 Live life as if it were a s-s-s-song …'
"'Stop!' they shouted. 'Start over! You m-m-m-made a mistake, R-R-R-Roscoe. Start from the b-b-b-beginning again!'" Mr. Halsey

swung his legs vigorously, nodding and slapping his thighs. "Oh, I was in trouble. I was absolutely struck dumb." He started to laugh. It was an insistent, high-pitched laugh, like the barking of a small dog. "One of the boys, who was by this time pretty excited, unhooks my belt, undoes my pants …" I was aghast at his telling me this. "… and in a minute my trousers and undergarment were around my ankles!"

He was laughing so hard now, that his face was red. "Oh, how funny it was!" he gasped. "'Come on, Roscoe, read your poem now. No mistakes! This should get you in the mood!' Ha, ha, ha! Oh, my!" He affected to be unable to speak for a moment, overcome by laughter. In a few seconds he continued.

"I tell you, I was absolutely struck dumb! Can you picture it? This pitiful little creature that I was, with my chubby belly and my eyes probably bugged out. We won't mention the pathetic condition of the underdeveloped rest of me—" I looked away, horrified. "—standing there, trying to say something, my mouth open like some kind of dumb fish! … They were patient, I'll say that for them. They must have had me standing in this state a good half an hour—"

I felt sick. As much as I disliked Mr. Halsey, perhaps *because* I disliked him, because he had the kind of personality he had, I almost couldn't tolerate knowing this had happened to him.

"Well, mercifully, Jean finally started to cry, and that intimidated them, I suppose, because they immediately let her go, and me too, but not before they removed my pants from around my ankles and tossed them onto the points of a tall chain-link fence that surrounded the school yard, so that I had to climb up it, like a monkey, to get them." He shook his head again. "What do you think of that, Miss Bradley? There's ridicule for you."

He seemed to expect me to say something. Finally I said, "Did that really … happen to you?" He raised his eyebrows.

"Oh, look at you. Don't be so solemn. That was no tragedy, far from it! Look where it got me! Today, I'm a teacher. Not to boast, but there's no point in being falsely modest; every single day I use our beautiful English language fluently, even poetically, I have to admit, to teach this same beautiful language to young minds who may never get such exposure to it from any other source again. And it's because of just such experiences as I've recounted to you. I don't mean to imply that by some miracle I was suddenly able to overcome my stuttering after that incident, but believe me, it made a strong and lasting impression on me which, little by little, spurred me on to work hard and eventually, through sheer determination, to solve my problem."

"I think I'd die if that happened to me. That shouldn't happen to *anyone*—" I stopped. I wondered if he knew I had meant to say, "Not even to *you*."

He got up from the desk and busily began to put papers in his shiny, black briefcase.

"Sometimes you have to be pushed to meet the challenges of adversity," he said brusquely. I watched him gathering his things together. I wanted desperately to leave now, but was held by a feeling that there was something I had a duty to say. I stalled.

"I'm sorry Jean didn't get to read the poem herself, instead of how it happened, Mr. Halsey. She probably would have liked it."

He didn't reply.

"What happened to her?" I asked.

He continued to pack his case. He put his fountain pen and sharpened pencils side-by-side in their slots and tucked his grade book and ruler in separate compartments. He neatly stacked his folders and papers. After sorting them in some obscure order, he re-sorted them as if he'd made a mistake. He stayed bent over his task as he answered me in a bright, genial voice.

"Oh, good lord, of course she avoided me from then on. What would you expect?"

"That's too bad," I said.

He was silent for a moment as he closed his case and laid it flat on the desk. Then he gave me a sidelong look. His mouth was curled up in its familiar sneer, cheeks lifted to narrow the hooded eyes, and a little of his teeth showing.

This expression, intimidating as it was, wouldn't have been so awful had it not been overlaid by a tremulousness that subtly shook him, face and body. It reminded me of a large rat I once saw clutching onto a bit of driftwood in the ocean at the end of a jetty. The rat's heart beat visibly under its wet plastered-down fur, and its eyes glittered with desperation. I had reached out with a stick I was carrying. I tried to hook the driftwood with it and bring the rat in closer so it could hop onto the jetty, but the rat bared its teeth at me, and I was afraid.

Mr. Halsey seemed to be waiting for me to add to my remark.

"Jean was probably just embarrassed," I murmured.

"No doubt," he replied. "It's natural. I don't blame her at all." He placed his hands on the briefcase and leaned across the desk toward me. "As much as your charitable heart bleeds for young Roger," he said, "do you see yourself actually being … *friends* with the boy? Especially now?" he added, and showed his teeth again.

I didn't know how to respond. If I said yes, I would be obliged for as long as I was under Mr. Halsey's scrutiny—the rest of the school year—to show Roger a conspicuous and artificial friendliness I didn't feel. If I said no …

"I don't know," I replied, lowering my eyes. "I could try." I continued to look down in the silence that followed and thought, when can I go home?

Then a small dark spot appeared on the black leather surface of his briefcase, exactly between his hands. Another appeared before he turned quickly away, raised his hand to his face, brushing it lightly with his sleeve, and began erasing the board. I stared at the spots as if they were drops of blood. As if I had happened on an accident, not knowing what to do.

I was desperate to leave but still felt there was something I must say, something missing from our conversation, and now it seemed even more important. What I wanted to say was, "Don't take it out on Roger, Mr. Halsey, or on *anybody*. Don't take it out on anybody." But there were those dark spots on his briefcase. It confused me to feel so much pity and so much contempt at the same time.

I seemed to despise the man more than I ever had. If I, a young girl, could see the simple correspondence between his childhood misery and the choice he had made to pass it on to others, how could he, a grown man, not see it too? How could he not see himself in Roger Nyles and take pity?

But I couldn't get the words out. Instead, I said, "I'll be prepared to talk about my poetry tomorrow, Mr. Halsey."

With his back still to me, he said, "Good. We'll look forward to it, Elizabeth. Well, go along."

I almost made my escape then, but something about his voice stopped me. It didn't sound quite so theatrical, so artificial. All of a sudden there was just the smallest hint of genuineness to it. Or maybe his back being to me gave me the courage to try to say what was on my mind.

I said, "That terrible thing that happened to you, Mr. Halsey, it seems like you would understand what Roger feels and not … not … hurt him."

He turned around. The sleepy lizard was back.

"Miss Bradley," he said, "brains and self-importance are your crowning characteristics. You don't have beauty. You don't even have a kind of beauty. You imagine yourself to be unique, like a character out of a book, don't you? You think you have a special sensitivity that sets you apart from everybody else, don't you? You see yourself as a heroine, but you aren't. All you are is an ungainly, self-dramatizing adolescent girl who doodles her absurd little drawings in her notebooks. You're no Jane Eyre, Miss Bradley. All you've got is brains and self-importance. I'm only saying this for your own good. Everything you think or say or do looks foolish because you are so conscious of yourself. Why don't you go home now and prepare to show us how very much you know about poetry."

I turned and walked to the back of the classroom, shaking, hot in the face and cold in the stomach, hardly able to see through a film of tears. As I went out the door he called to me genially, "And don't get yourself so upset about a little handkerchief."

I finished the rest of the school year in Mr. Halsey's class by maintaining a cold, polite formality. I stopped raising my hand or responding to his questions, and he, with unassailable objectivity, continued to put "S" for Superior on all my essays and tests.

It wasn't necessary to decide how friendly to become with Roger Nyles because he never returned. None of my classmates asked about him or even mentioned the incident.

At some point—when, I couldn't say—I created a myth to explain Roger's disappearance. I reasoned that, by coincidence, the day he chose to defy Mr. Halsey was the very day his family was to move out of town. He went to a new city and a new school, where he started over with a teacher who was indifferent to the use of handkerchiefs. He learned to read better than anyone in the class and went on to be a star athlete in high school. Later, and for many years afterward, I believed that someone had told me this about him.

Hugger and Thug

IVADEL MURPHY tasted blood in her mouth and smelled earth mold where her nose was pressed into the damp spring grass. A chickadee landed and hopped among the dandelions a few feet from her face. It looked her in the eye and appeared to speak to her in a kind and compassionate voice—not the typical "chickadee dee dee" but a soothing "sweetie, sweetie, sweetie," like words you might say to a child.

Ivadel watched the bird numbly for a few seconds. She felt cold all over and her whole body trembled from the inside. She thought, "Thank God the young women didn't see me like this. Only the children saw, and they didn't know what they were seeing."

Her own children told her she could have been an artist. They praised her for the little animals she fashioned from walnut shells and pine cones picked up on her nature walks, and for the decorative caps and blankets she had knitted for her grandchildren. They reminisced about the clever voices and pantomimes and puppet shows she used to entertain them with when they were young.

"You *are* an artist!" her children declared. And one day, after Ivadel had been retired six months from her job as a teller at the First Central Village Bank, she found herself staring at her hands and thinking with some excitement, "My children are right."

How many times at her teller's window had she looked at these hands, passing bills across the counter, and felt a twinge of shame at what she saw: bulging blue veins, thinning, papery skin, age spots.

But now, after she had cleaned out her bureaus and closets for the first time in more years than she liked to admit, and inserted piles of loose photos chronologically into albums, and delivered to the Goodwill those dusty boxes of jigsaw puzzles she and her late husband had often pieced together, she sat down and looked at her hands again with new eyes.

This time she saw in them a future with opportunities instead of years passing, and she rose and went directly to her sewing room, where she opened a trunk of fabrics and bric-a-brac. She plunged her hands into the calicos, the acetates, the faux furs and velvets, and poured out a tin box full of buttons as diverse in color and size as seashells on a beach, letting them sift through her fingers.

In the following weeks, she went to the library and checked out books, attended shows and conferred with the performers. She decided definitely to perform solo. The idea of managing single-handedly appealed to her. And she might earn a little income. Maybe even a *decent* income—who knew?

She would start small with only two puppets, acting out simple tales with plain messages: slow but steady wins the race, make hay while the sun shines, good overcomes evil. There would be satisfaction in delivering the old values which children were so much in need of today.

At her kitchen table, she sat through the late winter absorbed in the act of creation. When the light faded, she would look up at the clock and think, 5:00 P.M., where did the time go?!

She wanted to make a truly scary villain, so she gave the first puppet a mouthful of teeth, which she built from styrofoam packing peanuts she'd found in an empty gift box. The gaping incisors, like snaggly stalactites and stalagmites, each took an hour to build, no two exactly alike. Some she painted a lurid yellow, some a dirty gray. She glued them on to the open mouth of an old oven mitt. After the glue dried, with her thumb in the bottom part and her four fingers in the top, she could make the teeth ripple menacingly with each opening of the puppet's jaws. To complete it, she inserted a green velveteen tongue and made it loll carnivorously to one side. After that she sewed thick, glowering eyebrows on the face, and below these she glued buggy plastic eyes that she had found at a hobby shop. They opened and shut, and on the whites she painted bloodshot lines with red enamel.

Then she turned her attention to the design of the other puppet, her hero. Intelligent trickster or good-hearted innocent? She considered this question for several days. A photo of her one-year-old granddaughter provided the answer. In the picture, the little girl stared with frank astonishment at her own reflection in a mirror. This was the inspiration for the puppet's endearing saucer eyes. Ivadel left just a sliver of white below the iris to suggest trustfulness and wonder. She constructed her hero as a glove puppet with arms so it could wear clothes and manipulate props. The two characters she named Hugger and Thug.

For the rest of the winter, Ivadel prepared for her first performance. She bought black pants, turtleneck, and shoes, and a length of sheer black nylon to drape over her face. She made a black apron with large patch pockets for keeping props handy, and a waist-level stage to stand behind, constructed from accordioned cardboard attached to wooden stakes that could be pushed into the ground. She stapled cardboard bushes and trees to the stage and painted them in vivid colors. Finally, she made a lightweight wooden sandwich board announcing in large capital letters "A TALE OF HUGGER AND THUG" featuring a picture of the two puppets.

When the props were finished, she practiced her voices and

rehearsed the play, the simple story of Hugger's persistent efforts to befriend Thug, and Thug's constant attempts to make a meal of Hugger.

In early June, Ivadel was ready for a trial run. Her first venue would be a suburban park close to her home. The park had a pastoral feeling about it. There were graceful rolling hills, a duck pond, picnic tables under a stand of old sycamore trees, a little playground. Best of all, just out of hearing of the picnic and play areas, there was a secluded natural amphitheater—a stretch of flat grass backing onto a pine grove that faced a gently sloping hillside.

On the sunny day she visited, Ivadel saw a troop of a dozen preschoolers—three- and four-year-olds—brought to the park by two chaperones, a dark-haired young woman in her early twenties and a blond, tanned high school-aged girl. The two led the children in pairs through the park gate, each child holding onto a colored string attached to a length of rope. Ivadel thought they made a pretty little parade, the dark-haired young woman strolling purposefully ahead, a gym bag full of equipment banging against her hip, the children in bright and pastel-colored tee-shirts and shorts, and on their small feet oversized running shoes. At the end of the line, cheerfully herding the stragglers, came the blonde teenager, wearing Day-Glo capris and a tank top that exposed her slim, tan midriff. Just in front of her, a little boy in red shorts was vigorously yanking on his string, setting off a tugging match with his partner.

"Daryl, hold on nicely," said the blonde high school girl. She lay a restraining fingertip on the boy's arm. He stopped yanking and switched to jumping along on both feet. The girl put hands on his shoulders to check his vertical motion. "We're almost there," she said. Ivadel smiled. Her youngest daughter had been born with the same irrepressible energy.

The children trotted eagerly toward the playground, big tiger-, puppy- and bear-backpacks bouncing. A breeze carried their cries and laughter to the top of the hill where Ivadel stood. She watched the children break ranks and disperse in two directions, half of them running to the playground and the other half to the duck pond. The dark-haired young woman dropped her bag in the grass and hurried to the water's edge in time to steer the children away from it.

Once the children had wriggled out of their backpacks, the chaperone dispensed pieces of bread to each child. A mob of quacking ducks was already converging onto the grass. The children—all but one timid girl, who hung back and clung to the attendant's hip—scattered the bread and screamed in delight as the ducks darted around their ankles.

Predictably, the little boy in red shorts rushed the birds, sending them waddling and flapping out of reach. He threw all of his pieces of bread high in the air—impressively high for such a little boy—and watched the birds swoop after them. Then he picked crusts off the ground and fired them at the ducks. He screamed with laughter to see the bread bounce off the head of one and be snatched from the air by another. "Don't scare them, Daryl," urged the high school girl. "Stand quietly and they'll come to *you*."

Ivadel thought, not without amusement, that Daryl would be a handful.

She came the next day—Wednesday—at noon, and there they all were again, this time eating sack lunches at the picnic tables. Ivadel strolled across the playground and made her proposal to the chaperones.

"That would be awesome!" said the high school girl. The dark-haired young woman agreed.

"We come here from ten to two everyday if the weather's good," she said. "They take a twenty-minute nap right after lunch at twelve-thirty. So one o'clock would be a good time for a show, when they're a little more quiet."

Ivadel stayed for a while to watch the children play and to get a feel of the park. It seemed that this time—around midday in the middle of the week—the park was deserted except for the pre-schoolers. There would be no competition from shouting soccer players or people whistling for their straying dogs. She arranged to return the next day at one o'clock to "premiere" her show in the sylvan amphitheater.

On Thursday, Ivadel arrived dressed in her black outfit and carrying puppets and props in her pockets and pulling her stage and sandwich board in a cart. The young chaperones gave her a few minutes to prepare before bringing the children down. Ivadel wasn't surprised at her slight nervousness. It was natural. She gave herself a little pep talk and took some calming breaths.

Then she blew a tune on a kazoo to let them know she was ready, and the two assistants led the children down and helped settle them in the grass on the hillside. The shy little girl put a thumb in her mouth and climbed onto the blonde attendant's lap.

Ivadel introduced her puppet characters. She knew that children of three and four were easily frightened by puppet and cartoon villains, so she showed them how she had made Thug's teeth and sewn the lolling tongue. She demonstrated several possible voices for Thug before speaking in the oily sneer she had chosen for him. The children's eyes widened and mouths opened. A few of them got to their knees to scoot closer. Even the timid child left the blonde girl's lap and stood up for a better view.

Ivadel's nervousness quickly evaporated and was replaced by euphoria. She had set out to do this thing and now, here she was, doing it. She donned her black veil.

In a full, confident voice she started, "Once upon a time . . . " and soon Hugger and Thug were drawing squeals and laughter from the audience of children kneeling and sitting cross-legged in the grass. Only the boy in the red shorts—Daryl—found it hard to sit. He pulled out tufts of grass and scattered them in the air. He turned himself into a log and began rolling down the hillside, knocking into other children. The dark-haired young woman picked him up firmly and set him on her lap, where he slumped for a few seconds before he wriggled from her arms, broke and ran down the hill, veering off toward the duck pond. The attendant got to her feet and gave chase. Through the thin black veil, Ivadel saw her catch up to him and capture his hand as he seemed about to take a dive into the water. The young woman knelt by his side and spoke closely into his ear. He shook his head vigorously. The two stood then, watching the ducks together.

Ivadel felt briefly let down. But really, she thought, if eleven of the twelve children are engrossed, why should she criticize herself over one rambunctious child?

In any case, she was soon absorbed in the antics of her own characters, whose well-timed, coordinated movements and distinct interpretations of their roles astonished her. Hugger hopped about with a naturally manic cheerfulness, and Thug undulated its long neck and raised the corners of its mouth in impressively hideous grins. The children were thoroughly engaged.

"Look out, Hugger!" they screamed as the evil puppet crept up from behind and opened its cavernous mouth. Hugger bent down suddenly to smell a flower, and Thug tumbled, teeth first, against the trunk of the cardboard tree. The children shrieked with laughter. One or two stood up and pointed.

Glowing with success, Ivadel barely registered the sound of a motorcycle or motor bike driving up somewhere beyond the crest of the hill. She did catch a glimpse of the blonde girl standing up and shading her eyes to look toward the sound. The girl made a quick survey of the children, seemed satisfied that they were under control and, running her fingers through her hair, climbed to the top of the hill and out of sight. The timid child, by this time, was caught up in the puppet show and scarcely noticed her departure.

Ivadel stepped out from behind the stage. Hugger put both hands into one of the big patch pockets on Ivadel's black apron.

"Can you guess what there is in this pocket?" asked the puppet. The children called out various answers. One girl said, "*Poo* poo!" in a loud voice, and the others giggled. A sturdy, solemn boy in the front row got up and came forward to take a closer look.

"No," said Hugger. "Better not look yet. It's a surprise for my friend, Thug!"

"I know what it is!" exclaimed the little boy.

"Do you?" said Hugger. "But you can keep it a secret because you're a big boy, aren't you?"

"I'm three," he announced, holding up three fingers, and sat down again.

"Thug is *not* your *friend*!" another child warned Hugger, earnestly.

"No?" said Hugger. "I thought he was my very *best* friend."

"Thug is a *monster*!" cried the child.

The timid girl, still standing, was looking apprehensive again and starting to cast her eyes around for the blonde chaperone.

Ivadel stopped the performance and took off her black veil. "Remember, children, Thug is not a *real* monster," she said. She tucked Hugger into her pocket, removed Thug from her hand, and held the puppet up. "See? It's only a puppet."

The sturdy little boy in front shouted, "He *is* real! He's a bad Ninja! I saw him on TV!"

"No," repeated Ivadel, "it's just a puppet." Looking in the direction of the shy little girl, she said, soothingly, "Thug is made of soft, soft cotton!" She stroked Thug's neck. "Do you want to come and feel how soft it is?" The child put her thumb in her mouth again and shook her head fearfully, but the sturdy boy promptly marched across the strip of grass separating Ivadel from her audience and bopped Thug in the teeth.

"Got you!" he crowed and did a little dance as he walked back to his place, where he sat down. The other children tittered. "Got you!" they mimicked, and Ivadel said, "Oh! Poor Thug was only pretending to be a monster and now its lovely teeth are all wobbly." She put the puppet back on her hand and shook Thug's teeth to make them bounce against each other. The children laughed, and even the timid girl took a few tentative steps closer.

Ivadel drew the black veil over her face again and took Hugger from her pocket.

"Now where were we?" she said. "Oh, I remember. Thug was just about to take a nap." Ivadel stepped back behind the stage again.

Thug lay down under the tree and fell asleep, heaving loud, congested snores.

Hugger pulled out a giant yellow toothbrush with red bristles that Ivadel had made from a wooden hair brush.

"Guess what I'm going to do?" confided Hugger, in a low voice. "I'm going to sneak up while Thug is sleeping and brush his teeth for him. These snaggly old teeth really do need cleaning, don't you think?"

"Don't do it!" "He'll eat you!" yelled the children.

"I don't think he'll eat me, because he's my friend."

Hugger began to brush the teeth, but every time Thug snored, Hugger was blown backwards. The children howled and clapped.

Absorbed in manipulating the brush and timing the snores and double takes, Ivadel was caught a bit off guard when the timid little girl suddenly ran down to the stage and touched the teeth of the mouth puppet. She screamed with excitement, and ran back to her place, clutching her hands together.

Following suit, another little girl, in the front row, darted forward and touched the puppet, too.

"Uh oh!" Ivadel improvised, speaking directly to the audience as Hugger. "If Thug wakes up, he'll never let me finish brushing his teeth, will he? Let's be very, very quiet!" She put the puppet's hand to its lips. "Shh," said Hugger, "shh." And the puppet turned its head back and forth to look at all the children. "Can you help me? Can everybody say 'shh'!"

"Shhhhh!" "Shhhh!" "Shhhh!" On all sides the children made the sound, imitating her gesture with fingers to lips. Their shushing mingled with the gentle rustling of pine branches in the trees overhead. Within a few seconds the children were calm and attentive again.

Somehow, Ivadel thought to herself, she knew instinctively how to handle and engage the children. What she had done was so simple and spontaneous. It was a power she hadn't realized she possessed, and she felt rather thrilled by it. She wished the dark-haired young woman had been close enough to see, but she was still down by the duck pond supervising the child in the red shorts. Ivadel looked up toward the top of the hill. The blond high school girl was leaning against a boy of her age astride a motor scooter. The two appeared deep in conversation.

Hugger broke into an unrehearsed little song and dance. "Hush, hush, hush, while I brush, brush, brush!" Ivadel sang from beneath her veil, and a few of the children jumped up and capered in imitation before settling down again. "Now … " said Hugger, "I'll finish brushing my friend's snaggly, jaggly teeth. But don't forget … " The puppet put a hand to its mouth and all the children said, "Shhhh!"

Ivadel had not dropped Thug's character, in spite of the distractions, and now the villain yawned and smacked its lips, rolled over onto its other side and gave a loud snore. The children laughed. Hugger picked up the oversized brush and approached the sleeper carefully.

"Shhhh!" whispered the children, "Don't wake him up." Thug's head lifted and the bugged eyes flopped open. The children squealed, "Look out!" "He's waking up!" "Look out!" With a roar, Ivadel opened Thug's jaw and shook its wobbly teeth, then closed the jaw again on Hugger's right arm. Her fourth and little fingers inside Hugger's left arm curled around the brush handle and pulled.

"Let go, Thug!" protested Hugger. From the audience, children cried, "Let go, Thug!" One of them stood and declared, "I hate that Thug!" The two puppets pulled each other several times back and forth across the stage with loud shouts, and the brush accidentally slid from Ivadel's fingers and fell to the ground.

The sturdy boy promptly strode forward, snatched up the brush, and whacked Thug hard on the neck with it, delivering a jarring blow to Ivadel's wrist.

Ivadel drew her hand abruptly back. "No, no!" she admonished the little boy, more sharply than she intended. He promptly responded by hitting the puppet on the head, stinging Ivadel's knuckles. Trying to recover herself, she said, "*Nobody* hits the mighty Thug!"

She realized immediately that this was the wrong thing to say. Another child took up the challenge, stepping forth and punching Thug in the mouth, bending Ivadel's hand back and sending a shooting pain through her little finger. "*I* hit him for you, Hugger!" said the girl, giggling. Then she grabbed at Hugger, trying to pull the puppet off Ivadel's hand.

Ivadel closed her fist around the puppet and clutched the hem of Hugger's garment with her other hand, which was still inside

Thug's mouth. The child cried, "Don't eat my friend!" and slapped at Thug again, then tried to pry its jaws from around Hugger's neck.

As Ivadel bent down to struggle with the little girl, a bobby pin that fastened the black veil caught in the girl's hair and pulled it. "You hurt me!" the child cried, and punched the cardboard backdrop that hid the lower half of Ivadel's body.

Ivadel stumbled backward, her veil falling around her face in folds, obscuring her view. She tried to pull the veil straight, but several other children, having crossed the grass to crowd in close, were grabbing at her wrists and hands, trying to take possession of the puppets.

"Children!" she said, shrilly, "Hugger and Thug need to rest. Let them alone, now. They're very tired!" Through the doubled veil it was hard for her to see if the two attendants had returned. Ivadel tried to calm her shaking voice. "Sit down, everybody," she said. "Sit down quietly. We can't go on with the story until everyone sits!"

From behind her, a child reached up and grasped the corners of her veil, inadvertently stretching the nylon tight across her throat. For a moment she couldn't breathe. Clutching at the fabric, she was pushed again in the chest by the shy little girl and almost lost her balance.

She grasped the veil, wrenched it from her throat, and searched the hillside for the chaperones. The high school girl stood with her back to the spectacle below, but at the sounds of the children, she turned her head and glanced momentarily toward the scene. Apparently all she saw was the children crowded around the puppeteer, because she smiled and returned to her conversation. The young woman with the misbehaving boy was nowhere in sight.

Something prevented Ivadel from calling out. She didn't remember the teenaged girl's name and somehow couldn't bring herself to cry: "Girl! Girl!" or "Help me!" Then she was pushed again and she went down, the cardboard stage falling on top of her.

The children swarmed over her. The shy child picked up the glove puppet and sat down on Ivadel's chest with it, pushing the cardboard against her breasts and shaking the puppet in her face. The girl was probably no more than three years old, but she was solidly built and heavy. "I'm Hugger! I'll kiss you," she cried, excitedly. She leaned in close and pressed the puppet to Ivadel's mouth. Another child, imitating the first, fell on her, too, digging her knees into Ivadel's stomach. The sturdy boy wrenched Thug off Ivadel's hand and ran wildly around and around the group, swinging the puppet by the neck, like a lariat. Suddenly one of the children found the wooden hairbrush again and threw it in the air. It came down on Ivadel's forehead.

The impact and the sound of it striking her skull stunned her. In a panic to get up, she grabbed the shy girl's arm and tried to twist her off, but another child picked up the brush and began to bounce the stiff bristles against Ivadel's teeth. "Brush, brush, brush," she sang.

"Stop it!" Ivadel screamed at her. The child frowned and smacked the brush hard against her cheekbone and Ivadel fell back. Another child joined the heap and the three, giggling, began to bounce on her chest and stomach, knocking the wind out of her and driving the edge of the cardboard into her larynx. Desperately, she arched her back and pushed with all her strength. The children tumbled off, squealing with delight.

Ivadel struggled to rise up onto her hands and knees, and in an instant, half a dozen children were trying to clamber onto her back to ride her. One straddled her neck. "Horsey! Horsey!" he shouted. He took hold of her hair for reins and yanked her head back. Three others, astride her in their oversized running shoes, kicked at her arms and legs. "Giddy up, horsey!" they ordered. She tried to crawl out from under them, but her arms collapsed beneath the weight and she fell again, cracking an elbow against the wooden sandwich board, which had been knocked over and was lying on its side.

There came a rushing sound in her ears, mingled with the children's giggles and laughter and the rhythmic thud on the earth of the sturdy boy still galloping round and round. Ivadel's nose was shoved into the grass and she felt her lip split against her teeth as her mouth struck a rock. Another blow of the wooden brush landed on her temple, but she had no breath left to gasp at it. Her vision grew dark and she thought she heard bells ringing.

Then suddenly the crushing weight lifted from her back. One after another, the children peeled off and ran away. Their eager shouts grew more remote, and the young woman's thin voice called, "Get your quarters out for ice cream!" The melodious bells tinkled for a few moments and then stopped.

There was silence.

Ivadel tried and failed to shift her weight off the edge of the crumpled stage which had somehow got under her and was pressing into her ribcage. A shuddering tremor had commenced deep inside her body like an old, out-of-tune engine laboring there. Then, as if from a distance, she became acutely aware of herself on the ground, quivering like a wounded animal. She had the strange sensation of standing over herself, thinking, this old woman died and there was nothing left of her but a heap of black clothes.

Half of her face was pressed into the ground, but the other half caught a glimpse of the sky. It was the garish blue color of an artificially tinted postcard. It hurt her eye to look at it. Inches from her face lay a green leaf mottled with red. She tasted blood in her mouth. The smell of dank earth filled her nostrils.

Just then a chickadee landed in the grass next to where she lay. It was so close she could see her face reflected in its eye. It cocked its head and looked at her for a few moments. Strangely gentle sounds issued from its throat.

The thought occurred to her: "If it hadn't been for the boyfriend on the motorcycle and the little boy in the red shorts, the young

women would have seen me like this. Oh thank God they didn't."
Then she thought, "But if they'd been here, it wouldn't have happened. They would have known what to do. Even my own grown
children would have known what to do."

She moved her limbs one at a time. When she found that no
bones had been broken, she got slowly to her feet. Without waiting
for a spell of dizziness to pass, she stumbled about, picking up the
debris of the puppet show and stuffing it into the cart. She felt too
weak to carry the sandwich board and left it where it lay. Pulling
the cart, she exited the park by way of a small tunnel that led out
to the street. At home, she pushed the cart into an unused closet in
the garage and shut the door on it. She thought, "Only the children
saw, and they didn't know what they were seeing."

Not to Worry

i. Worry cops

MOST OF MY LIFE, I've had the two habits of worrying and talking to myself, often at the same time. For example, after I used mustard from a glass jar that fell on the floor but did not break, I started to worry that I might have missed some little splintering of glass somewhere in the mustard. So then I discussed this possibility at length with an imaginary listener. What if I swallowed glass, and it's going to lacerate my stomach?! How would they test for that? Probably not an x-ray. Maybe an ultrasound or MRI. Oh, not an MRI! All that electromagnetic radiation! And if the tests did find glass cuts, I wonder if the doctors would think I'd tried to kill myself and ought to be committed for psychiatric evaluation.

So I was standing around in my kitchen, yammering away about this, blah, blah, blah, blah, and suddenly I just stopped, and I thought, Why am I talking about this? And who am I talking to? And immediately the answer came to me: I was talking to the worry police. The worry police exist to enforce an ordinance that says I'm required to worry at least seventy-five percent of my waking hours.

And all of a sudden I can *see* these cops. It's two guys. Standard blue uniforms, paraphernalia hanging off them—Tasers, radios, guns. These guys are about forty years old, medium height, medium build, beginnings of a paunch. And I realize that even though they're only forty years old, they've been on the Force for at least sixty-three years, because I'm sixty-nine and I started this worrying when I was about six.

There's a good cop and a bad cop. Good cop calls me "Ma'am."

"Ma'am, are you aware that you have not been worrying for the last five minutes?"

"Really? No, I'm sorry, I didn't realize that."

The bad cop is stone-faced. He dispenses with the niceties.

"Actually we clocked you at five minutes and forty-five seconds worry-free."

"Oh gosh, I'm sorry. I just wasn't thinking."

"Exactly."

Good Cop says, "Ma'am, we need you to take an adrenaline blood level test. Would you please step back into your brain?"

Bad Cop takes the reading, curls his lip.

Good cop says, "Ma'am, your adrenaline level needs to be at least double this number."

Bad Cop says, "You want to roll up your sleeve?" He *cuffs* me! "Systolic 130, diastolic 75." He shakes his head.

Me: "Not bad enough?"

He sneers. "Not even in the ball park."

Me: "But—"

Good Cop says, "Ma'am, we're just here to see that you worry to the full extent of the law."

Here's an example of how diligent these cops are:

I was walking on the rubberized surface of the children's playground, and I started to imagine some conscientious citizen criticizing me for it. "Can't you walk on the pavement like every other adult? If everyone takes a shortcut across the playground, it will constantly have to be re-surfaced at tax-payers' expense!" So I explain that I suffer from chronic back pain, and those few measly seconds on that soft surface give me a little relief. Conscientious citizen says, "Really? Back pain?" And I'm starting to fume! Mind you, none of this conversation has actually taken place. But my cops are beaming over this. They take full credit.

Earlier that same day I had to catch a bus to get to my office to prepare for a class I was teaching. On my way to the bus stop, a neighbor came up to chat. I excused myself, explaining I was a little late and I had to catch a bus. I caught the bus. But all the way to work, I obsessed about what *would* have happened if I'd missed the bus and had to walk into that class unprepared and face twenty-eight disdainful undergraduates, all of whom would have thought I was wasting their time. My cops high-fived each other on that one. They are so good!

They're so good they even follow me when I'm taking a walk. Like the President, followed, 24/7 by secret security agents, I have to learn to ignore the implicit message: "We're here because there's a distinct possibility that you're going to die." Lately, though, I've taken to glancing back at them. "Hi guys." They hate it when I do that.

But they had me waking up at 5:00 a.m. to worry that if we had a storm, hypothetical golf ball-sized hail might destroy my roof before I could sell my house. It's *5:00 a.m.* and these cops are in bed with me! They have to spoon with each other for the three of us to fit.

Me: "Hey, you're in bed with me? That can't be comfortable for you."

Good Cop: "All in the line of duty, Ma'am."

Or I'll be in the shower. Relaxing. Enjoying nice hot water on my back. But then I'll think what if I slipped in the shower and conked my head and lay unconscious with water hitting my nose and my mouth. I could drown. And I say, "Hey, cops! I'm in the shower! Give me some privacy here!"

Good Cop: "Ma'am, vigilance trumps privacy."

"But following me into the *bathroom*?"

Bad Cop: "How do we know that shower won't calm you down?"

Good Cop: "Ma'am, think of it this way. If you aren't worrying, anything could be a surprise."

"But if I *am* worrying, anything could be a surprise. I can't be worrying about *everything*."

Bad Cop: "Don't be so sure."

Now, just between you and me, recognizing that it's the cops making me worry is actually making me worry less. And I'm starting to enjoy teasing them. Like maybe I'll go for a good long stretch of time worry-free, and then I'll have a minor unsettling thought like, what if my watch is slow and it's ten minutes later than I think it is. And I say, "Oh cops, you're back? I'd hate to report you for dereliction of duty, but, my worries ... they're getting kind of piddly."

Good Cop says, "Ma'am, no worry is too piddly."

You know, I started worrying about my worry cops because, on the one hand, when I *am* worrying, they're *working* so hard. They hardly ever get breaks! I feel sorry for them. On the other hand, if I'm not worrying, I feel guilty for letting them down.

The other day I asked them, "What do *you* worry about?" Well, it turns out that seventy percent of their worries are job-related. They worry that I'm not worrying enough.

That got me wondering: who are *their* enforcers?

Anyway, their worries are now realized. I *am* getting pretty complacent. And they've gotten so frustrated, that they put in for a transfer, and got it. Their new assignment is to convince Extreme Sports enthusiasts to fear death. I think that's going to be a very nice challenge for them.

So we've said our good-byes. I did make a little faux pas. I said, "Take it easy." Bad Cop glared at me. Good Cop said, "Ma'am, we know you didn't mean it like that." His parting words to me were: "Ma'am, Worry. Don't be happy." I replied, ambiguously, "Don't worry, I will."

ii. Stop me if I've told me this

SO AFTER MY Worry Cops got reassigned to a job instilling fear in Extreme Sports enthusiasts, I was relatively worry-free for a while. Then, with the inevitable encroachment of anxieties attending old age, in addition to life in a proto-fascist dictatorship led by a sociopath with dementia, my tranquility started to erode. I began to fill the void with repetitive internal narratives recited to fancied listeners. The following is a random sampling of my topics:

1) The scintillating tale of my thin hair, the fruitless search on line for barrettes that didn't slide off, and my ultimate decision to cut my hair so short I looked like a boy (or, more accurately, an old geezer), but at least I no longer have to mess with it.

2) A persuasive set of arguments as to why an imagined Trump supporter should see the light.

3) The saga of my back problems and a review of every treatment I've tried for the last thirty years, along with disgruntled assurances to some well-meaning but annoying, non-existent interlocutor that, no, really, there's nothing I haven't tried.

4) Detailed accounts of the myriad forms of voter suppression and erosion of First Amendment rights in the U.S., with a seamless segue into a historical analysis of the many ways our current political situation in 2019 resembles that of 1929 Germany.

5) The fascinating events that led to my getting an ulcer and the circumstances under which I might someday get another one.

6) The equally fascinating events that led to my coming down with pneumonia in October 2016 (or was it November? No, it was October. Oh, no wait, it *was* November because I came down with it the day after the election) and the circumstance under which I might get pneumonia again, i.e. the year 2020.

7) A detailed defense of the scientific evidence for human-created climate change, ending with the irrefutable challenge: If

you don't think people have anything to do with it, how do you account for the gray veil that blots out entire towns and cities as seen from a plane?

8) A comprehensive listing of preventatives (in descending order of effectiveness) that I employ to ward off migraines.

9) A recitation—to someone who might ask about my dietary habits—of an informative list of ingredients that make up the healthful breakfast I've eaten every day for two decades. (So far, no real person has ever asked me, but you never know.)

As you can imagine, such spell-binding narratives take up a lot of psychic space in my brain, especially since I seem to stream them on a feed-back loop. And until now I've never had the courtesy to preface my stories with, "Stop me if I've told me this" to which I could reply, "Well, you know, I think maybe I *have* heard this one before."

Then, just recently, I decided it was time to get tough with me. My stories were becoming like Norse sagas told around the synaptic fireside to generations of my brain cells. I really didn't need to hear these tales again.

So now, when my mind gets going—"The thing is, my hair has always been thin, but it's definitely thinner now that I'm—" I jump right in:

"This story, how many times have I told it to me?"

"Uh …"

"More than once?"

"Well, yes."

"More than five times?"

"Um …"

"Fifty? A hundred?"

"Probably at least that."

"Is this a story that I'm likely to forget if I don't tell it to me again?"

"Probably not."

(Definitely not.)

But within minutes: "The thing is, this ulcer wasn't the kind that can be cured with antacids because it was caused by—" I have to interrupt me again or I'll have me politely standing there for ages, forced to listen to this stuff until I can finally come up with an excuse to get away:

"I'd love to hear this story for the two hundred and twenty-sixth time, but I've got another thought coming in that needs my attention. Do I mind if I hear it sometime next year?"

"Oh, sure, it wasn't important anyway."

(Exactly.)

The thing is, I try not to bore actual people with these lengthy narratives, but for myself, I seem to think I've got nothing better to do than to let me endlessly yammer away with no chance to get a word in edgewise. Really it's so rude. I might have something else I'd like to think, but no, there's no back and forth. I don't know how to share the time.

So, this is my strategy. I've stopped being tactful. When I catch me starting another droning, internal anecdote, I just hold up a figurative hand and interrupt me by asking how often I've told me the story and whether it's crucial for me to hear it again. And guess what? It never is.

Priorities

i. Chicken Little

EVERYONE CALLED him "Chicken Little." It was a disparaging nickname. He had a perfectly good real name—Al—and was once second highest in the pecking order. But when he started warning everybody in the coop and the barnyard that the sky was going to fall, almost everyone mocked him and refused to listen to anything he had to say. With mathematical and scientific calculations he showed them how much lower the sky already was. They refused to consider his statistics.

They joked about his boring, bland personality, his lack of a sense of humor. In fact he was a rather handsome rooster with a deep, resonant voice, a calm demeanor, and a thoughtful, inquiring mind. Even those who agreed with him made little jokes about his "one-note" preoccupation. They seemed to find off-putting the sheer quantity of facts he knew about the sky and its impending fall.

He tried to describe the problem in lay terms that even a baby chick should be able to understand (the baby chicks actually did understand him, but by the time they became adults, it would be too late for them to be part of the solution).

Despite the mockery and dismissiveness of those around him,

he never stopped trying to convince others that it wasn't quite too late to prevent the sky from falling if they would only rally 'round.

The sky fell.

The ones who had thought it would not fall, who thought the falling sky idea was a political ploy or divine inevitability, who thought no one needed to do anything about the sky, did not exclaim, "Oh, what were we thinking? We were fools, idiots. You were right. We were wrong. Now we see it." They didn't exclaim those things. They didn't think those things. They were dead.

ii. Three wishes

DO YOU SOMETIMES imagine what you would choose if you could have three wishes about yourself? For me, number one would be to have thick, wavy hair. Number two, to no longer have bags under my eyes. And number three, to have a flat stomach.

And if only I had *four* wishes, I'd get rid of these frown lines ... or the lines on my upper lip. But ... maybe frown lines and lines on the upper lip *and* bags under the eyes could come under one category for wish number two, like ... no wrinkles. Then I could have all of that and for wish number three a flat stomach. But ... I'd sure like to get rid of this loose flesh on my upper arms and the backs of my thighs. Wait a minute, couldn't those two be subsumed under muscle tone? Actually a flat stomach comes under muscle tone, so I could have all of *those* under one wish. So okay, good muscle tone for number three, including tight upper arms, stomach, and backs of thighs. Yes. That works.

What am I thinking? I need to wish for a good *back*. Number three should be no back pain. A pain-free back. That has to be number *one*.

Okay. Start over. Pain free back number one, thick wavy hair number two. Number three, good muscle tone. And aren't wrinkles just a sign of poor muscle tone? I could throw in wrinkles under muscle tone: So, for number three: firm upper arms, stomach, backs of thighs, no under-eye bags, no wrinkles. Yes.

What about world peace, though? If I *had* the three wishes ... Yes, obviously, world peace has to be number one ... And an end to environmental degradation ... And the elimination of poverty. Well, there's your three wishes right there.

But, now, couldn't *those* three be boiled down to one wish?... What about an end to the abuse of power? An end to the abuse of power. That works! Peace, environment, poverty—taken care of in one wish.

Which leaves me with two personal wishes left out of the three. So, which ones? Okay, well, of course, getting rid of the back pain has to take priority, that's a given. So which of the other two? Muscle tone or thick wavy hair?

Thick wavy hair. No contest.

But it is *so* frustrating to be allowed only three wishes.

iii. Appalled but not surprised

DO YOU remember those old-fashioned aluminum ice cube trays that came with refrigerators in the '40s and '50s? You'd pull the lever up to loosen the ice cubes? Well, anyway, I was thinking about ordering an updated version of one of these online, and I found several; one looked good, made of stainless steel and priced at $19.95. But first I scanned some customer reviews, and I came across this one, written by "Appalled but not surprised." The review was found helpful by one hundred twenty-nine people. Maybe it will be helpful to you.

Here's what "Appalled but not surprised" wrote:

This loathsome abomination broke the first time I pulled the lever. The product description boasts that it's made of *'gleaming stainless steel.'* Is this some kind of practical joke? Oh yeah, it gleams all right. But, Oops! Don't *I* look foolish with that lever hanging from one hand, the tray from the other, and the dividers and ice cubes on the floor. *'Just like the old days,'* it says. Really? Which old days would those be? The days when itinerant quacks went around selling swamp water? I resent being deliberately enticed with abhorrent gimcracks that promise to bring back your most cherished memories of yesteryear and then trample on your heart while the corporation laughs all the way to the bank. *'Ha ha! Gotcha, you sentimental sucker.'* As a little girl, I was filled with pride when my parents let me pull the lever of the ice tray and pop out the ice for our lemonade. It worked so easily a five-year-old could operate it. My parents got good use out of those ice cube trays for fifty years, and I'd still be using them if they hadn't accidentally been sent off to the landfill with the old refrigerator. So I guess I'll have to keep using the hard plastic ice trays that practically sprain your wrists when you twist out even a couple of cubes. And no, forget about those automatic icemakers that foist off on you those pathetic half-moon slivers that melt as soon as they hit the liquid. I *had* looked forward to making the nice, substantial ice cubes I remembered from childhood. Was that just too much to ask? And now, when I send the despicable contraption back, I'll again have to pay the egregious 'shipping' cost and spend time and gas money getting it to a UPS outlet—a win-win for both companies but insufferable psychological and financial loss for me.

Well. This customer review *was* helpful. It kind of got me thinking about those small, everyday conveniences that we take for granted. You know what I mean? Like … oh, like, … for example, not having to cross the Mediterranean, packed into an overloaded inflatable raft, hanging on to babies and elderly parents to keep them from falling overboard. You know? Those little comforts of life? Like not having to stumble, freezing, wet, and terrified onto a beach where armed police greet you with buses and take you to a filthy, crowded detention center until they can ship you back to your country where you'll meet certain death?

It's those simple, old-fashioned conveniences that we've come to expect, like the original aluminum ice cube tray. Is it any wonder that "Appalled but not surprised" is outraged?

—All my belongings?
 —Every single one of them.
 —Even the clothes on my back?
 —Even those.

But in the end they let me keep the clothes on my back, for they (the world's poor) didn't want their children exposed to a wandering naked man.

They asked me,—Do you have a house?
 —No, *I said, truthfully.*
 —A roof over your head?
 —Yes, an apartment.
 —How many rooms has it?
 —Four rooms. Not including the kitchen and the bathroom.
 —So six rooms?
 —Well ... yes.
 —And how many people?
 —Just me.
 —Does your apartment have heat?
 —Yes.
 —And water that runs from a tap?
 —Yes.
 —And a toilet that flushes?
 —Yes.
 —Is electricity provided to your house?
 —Yes.
 —And do you have a car?
 —Yes.
 —More than one?

—No.

—Does your car have its own house?

—I suppose so. Yes.

—Is electricity provided to your car's house?

—Yes. Just a couple of outlets.

—How many things do you have that are operated with electricity?

—Well …

—Take your time to count.

—In the kitchen … eight. No, ten, including light fixtures. …In the bathroom … uhh …

—Take your time.

—In the bathroom, six. In the living room and dining room …

—We would offer you paper and a pencil to figure with if we had them, *one woman said politely.*

—Sixteen, I believe. And in the bedrooms … twenty.

—In all, fifty-two things that run on electricity. *She had done the calculations in her head.*

—Yes, I guess so.

—What articles of clothing do you own?

—Well, I have shirts, pants, jackets, shoes, socks, coats … underwear …

—Exactly how many of each?

—I'm not sure.

—You don't know?

—Not exactly.

—More than two?

—Yes.

—More than three?

—Yes.

—More than four?

—I think I only … I have four coats.

—Shoes?

—Maybe six or eight … Six, I think. Six pairs.

—You know that we can check.

—It could be eight, or possibly nine.

—And the other articles of clothing?

—I just don't know for sure.

—You don't know how many shirts and pants and jackets and socks you have? Or how much underwear?

—No, I don't.

—Do you have a job?

—Yes.

—At the place where you do your job, is there a roof over your head?

—Yes.

—And heat in the cold months?

—Yes.

—Protection from the sun in summer?

—Yes.

—How many miles must you walk to arrive at your job?

—Well, five miles, but …

—Are there any steep hills along the route?

—Yes, but …

—Must you carry any tools of your trade with you?

—No. Well, yes. My books and papers.

—How long does it take you to arrive there?

—Fifteen minutes.

—Only fifteen minutes?

—By car.

—By driving your car.

—Yes.

—And you always have enough gasoline to take you there?

—Yes, unless I forget to fill up.

—You forget about gasoline?

—Not often.

—How much food do you eat?

—I don't know how much in quantity, if that's what you mean, but I usually eat three times a day, moderate amounts. I try not to eat too much. I don't have snacks in between meals.

—You try not to eat too much?

—Yes.

—You mean it is difficult not to eat too much?

— … Sometimes.

—It is easy to eat too much?

—Well …

—You can see why it is your turn to give up all your belongings.

—Except the clothes on his back, *one of the others reminded her.*

—Except the clothes on your back. You see the reason?

I thought of my tall corner windows, how in winter the sunlight fell on the pages of my book and gilded the green tea in my glass. I thought of people with many houses and personal jets.

—It seems a little harsh, *I mumbled, lowering my eyes.*

—Yes, it is, it is so harsh, *she said, adding gently,*—and so bitter.

Bon Voyage

Y MOTHER'S forehead is like marble, cold from the mortuary refrigerator. Her hair is wet and stringy. Why would they wash the hair of someone soon to be cremated? If they were making an effort to clean her up for my sake, why didn't they dry it afterward and brush it out nicely?

I pity my mother for her cold marble forehead and wet, stringy hair. She sees her reflection in my eyes and says, Oh I look ghastly!

Don't worry about it, Mom, I say. You're supposed to look ghastly. It's nothing to feel self-conscious about. You've earned the right to look ghastly. You're dead.

But she doesn't believe me.

I'm dead? How could I be dead?

I don't know, Mom. You were supposed to live forever.

That's what I thought, too, she says. But here I am, dead.

Yes.

What happens next, I'm afraid to ask?

You'll be cremated.

Cremated! That doesn't sound good. Will it hurt?

No. Because you're dead.

Well, I'm glad of that. And afterward?

I don't know, Mom. Nobody knows. If you can, maybe you could try to get word back to me.

I'll try.

Well, I hate to leave you.

Why do you have to?

I guess there's just a time when you have to see your dead mother off and go home.

Well, thank you for coming. I'll miss you.

Will you? Because I'll miss you more than anything or anyone else in the world, and missing you will never stop and there will be nothing I can do about it. But that's selfish of me to say. You're the one about to leave this earth. I wish I could keep you company, Mom.

No. I wouldn't expect it of you. I'll be fine. I'm sure it will be okay. It will probably be quite interesting. Don't worry about me.

Mom is dressed in the clothes I brought over earlier, but at the last minute I take off her shoes—her dainty little low-heeled navy-blue pumps—and clutch them under my arm. She is lying—now shoeless—in a long cardboard box on a gurney. The undertaker lifts it easily into the oven.

Bon voyage, Mom says, as if I am the one taking the journey.

Write, I say, just to lighten the moment, and she promises to, if she has time.

A button is pushed and the door slides shut. I pull down the lever that starts the heat. The mechanism inside roars to life.

It takes about half an hour to reach the optimum temperature, says the undertaker.

It will be very noisy in there while she's waiting, I think. But maybe no noisier than being on an ocean liner when the engines rev up and the steam whistle blows and the people on board and on the dock, with the wind whipping their hair, shout their goodbyes, and the vessel begins to churn water and plough backward out into the open harbor, drowning the cries of the seagulls circling overhead.

If I'd Been Late

THE THING I remember about it is that if I hadn't gotten back with the car on time, Robert wouldn't have taken it out and he never would have run it off the road and got killed. If I'd just been twenty minutes late he would have gotten pissed off waiting and probably taken a ride with his buddy instead of driving himself, and he'd be alive today, and that's always bothered me because I was usually late for things. I was completely undependable. You could never count on me to be on time. So why on that one occasion did I bring the car back when I was supposed to? I forget where I was coming from. Where *was* I coming from? Not school. It was a Saturday, I'm pretty sure. You'd think I'd remember, but my memory is so fucked up. Probably from smoking marijuana for thirty years.

Oh, I do remember. I was over at Donny Neff's house trying to get him to sell me the pool table his folks gave him that wouldn't fit in any room in his house. But he wouldn't do it, and I guess that's why I got back on time, because I was disgusted with him and I just walked out. They didn't have a rec room or a heated garage for that pool table. It just sat there doing nothing except letting the cat sharpen its goddamn claws on it—the felt was all torn up. I told him he could play in our basement. My brothers had Friday night poker games down there, and there was still plenty of room for a table, with enough clearance to play the game. But he wouldn't do it. He was keeping it "in case." In case *what*, you fuckface? In case your tightfisted parents sell that crackerbox sometime in this millennium and move into a place with a decent rec room? Donny's father was chief accountant at Massenger and Stutzman in the City. He must've been making a bundle, but he probably pissed it away on booze.

But the thing is, if Donny had said yes, I would have gotten involved with casing out that table and figuring out how to get the legs off and maybe called up my brothers and told them to measure the clearance on the bend in our basement stairs—although, no, I wouldn't have called, because Robert would have hassled me to get the car home. But I would have hung out with Donny to haggle over the price, which would have taken a lot of time since he was such a selfish, petty bastard. But I was disgusted and so I said, fine, keep the damn table, let the cat rip it up. Use the shreds for kitty litter. Let your dad pile tax receipts from before the Depression on it. It's your loss if you can't see a good deal when it's under your nose, you stupid Neanderthal.

So I screamed out of there, burned rubber in his driveway. I drove even faster than I usually did, which was at cop-defying speeds, around those bends. Robert taught me where to slow down for the radar traps—no, wait—did they use radar back in the seventies? I don't think so. He just knew where the cops always waited. He could bring that Renault down from seventy to thirty in the blink of an eye without losing control.

That's another thing—I still don't see how he could have lost control on a straight, empty road in broad daylight enough to go off and hit a tree like that, square on. They said he had alcohol in his blood, but so what? He drove all the time with alcohol in his blood, and he never had an accident before, only fender benders in parking lots. *I* knew he had alcohol in his blood. Nobody had to tell me, *or* our parents. That didn't surprise them, I'm sure. Those were the days before these high penalties for DWI and all this bullshit about designated drivers. I mean, it's not bullshit, but I get kind of sick of it. Why don't they go after other people who cause accidents—the blue hairs who creep onto the highway at ten miles an hour, or these bigshots clipping their nose hairs in the rearview mirror while they drive their gas guzzlers a half a block to work? It wasn't the alcohol.

He was in his Air Force uniform. He just got home from basic training. His hair was really shaved—down to the skull practically, but he liked it that way. It was always hard for me to picture Robert putting up with that military discipline crap.

Maybe *that* was it. Once he was there, it drove him crazy to be told what to do all the time. Maybe when he got home, for a while he just went on a freedom binge but took it too far. They figured he was going around 100 mph when he hit the tree. So what? He took the Renault up to 100 mph a lot of times and never hit anything.

That tree hardly got hurt. Some splintered bark, otherwise just as solid and straight as always. It was a landmark around there, a *huge* mother. It would take three kids to get their arms around it. The car hit it and just kept going into itself like the rear of the car didn't realize the front of the car had stopped. It was all compressed like a beer can when you finish the drink and set the can upright on the floor and stomp it flat. But the tree was pretty much fine.

That's the thing, though, the tree had always been there. It wasn't like a surprise—hey, where did that tree come from, I wasn't expecting it, BLAM. And the Renault was the Renault. He'd been driving that car for three or four years. The speed was usual. Well, maybe not *usual*, but not completely out of the ordinary. And the alcohol—he probably had some alcohol in his blood *most* of the time—so what was different? I always go back to my not being late with the car. That was definitely unusual. I'm not saying I blame myself—how fucked up would *that* be? I'm supposed to see into the future and know my brother is going to smash head-on into a tree if I get the car home on time? I don't mean *that*, but it's so weird that the one time I'm not late—.

Actually, that wasn't the only thing that was unusual. The other thing was his enlisting in the Air Force. I was surprised when Robert enlisted. But then I was surprised when Keith let him go to the recruiting office alone.

Keith wouldn't join up. You'd think, being twins, they'd have gone in together, but Keith had no interest in it. He had no use for all that marching crap—yes *sir*, no *sir*, how many hundred push-ups would you like me to do, *sir*, so you won't call me a pussy in front of a platoon full of other terrified ass lickers? Keith would have killed himself before getting into that kind of shit. So. Yeah. Well, there you have it. Maybe. Nothing to do with anyone being on time or not on time. I don't know what kind of shit Robert got into in basic training. He just joked around about it. He made fun of the whole thing when he came home. And he said he was going back.

But maybe … I never thought about this before but … I wonder if not having Keith around could have had something to do with it. When I try to remember things the two of them did separately, I can't picture many. It wasn't like they were the Bobbsey twins, though. I mean, they didn't take craps together or brush each other's teeth. But everything that one of them got a kick out of, they *both* got a kick out of. Like those Friday night poker sessions. And everything that pissed them off—they rebelled against the same things. They got thrown out of Little League three times for cursing umpires. One time Robert called this old guy with his gut hanging out of his striped shirt a mother-fucking whore, and Keith called him an asshole "banster." They were eight years old. They didn't even know how to pronounce "bastard" or what it meant. That was a family story.

One way they *were* different, Keith was the one who kept Robert from going too far. They used to put me through a lot of shit until I got taller than they were and got some muscle. But when I was little, Robert would pin me down and tickle me or put a pillow over my face until I was almost passing out—I'd struggle like a madman. Or he'd yank my arm up behind my back and pull it practically out of the socket. But Keith would get him off me. I think Robert could have just kept on going until he killed me if Keith hadn't always stepped in. Once Robert started to get wild, he worked up this insane momentum like he had no control over it. But—this is my point—Keith was always around to stop him. I never remember Robert doing anything to me or getting into any trouble when Keith wasn't there to calm things down. Now that I think about it, Robert going into the Air Force was the first time they were really apart, I'm pretty sure. So maybe he had no one to keep him in line.

Shit, what am I saying? That's the whole goddamn point of the military—keep *everybody* in line. But he could take it from Keith. He never seriously fought with Keith. Everyone else he would fight like a son of a bitch, but if Keith said lay off, he laid off. What would they do to someone in the Air Force who couldn't lay off? But maybe that's why he went in to begin with. Maybe he got scared of himself. Maybe he needed discipline. Or wanted it.

Huh. Something I forgot about—Robert did hurt Keith one time. He broke his nose. I don't think he meant to do it. It was an accident. He was supposed to pull his punch, but he didn't. That was when people began to tell them apart. Keith's nose looked different from Robert's after it got broken.

When the hell did that happen? Their junior year in high school? Or senior year? Something like that, I don't know. Robert enlisted in '63, so it was somewhere around '62 or '61. Jesus, they could have *both* been killed if Keith had been in that car. I'd be brotherless now. Where *was* Keith that day? I'm thinking he'd gone off somewhere that afternoon. Yeah, because when we got the news, we had to go round him up. So that was a time when they did something apart. Even with Robert just home from training, they weren't all *that* inseparable. Dad tracked Keith down shooting baskets with some guys over at Georgy Enzle's house. Yeah, that's right.

Now I remember something. When I brought the car home, I asked Robert where Keith was, and he said he was at Georgy's. Or, he said he didn't *know*, he *thought* he was at Georgy's. Yeah, and I asked Robert why he wasn't there, too, and I think he said he'd been waiting for some Air Force buddy to call. He was going to take the Renault and go meet the guy. But I never heard afterward of any Air Force buddy—nobody from the Air Force called or showed up at the funeral after Dad told them Robert died.

Which brings me back to that idea I have. It's irrational, I know. If I hadn't been on time, maybe Robert would have walked over to Georgy's and shot baskets that afternoon instead of ramming himself into the trunk of a motherfucking tree. He and Keith could have been shooting hoops with a bunch of their buddies just like any other Saturday afternoon of their lives. Why did I have to choose that one afternoon to not be late bringing the goddamn car home? I wish I could get that out of my mind. Christ, that stuff's pointless to dwell on.

Later, Keith and I bought this land together, after we moved out here to the Midwest and flunked out of college. It was a very sweet spot for our little agricultural enterprise. Totally remote. We could easily stay off the grid. You can't imagine how much profit you can make from that shit. I built my house from all the money we made. Put all that crap in it—Persian rugs, paintings, first edition books. Bought cars, a big honking truck. I shouldn't tell you that, probably. I won't even say how much money we made in those days. Of course I pissed it all away. We quit that operation four or five years ago, around '95, '96. It got too risky. I've got zip income now. I can't even afford a tune-up on that fucking rust trap of a truck. My wealth went right down the toilet. But we still do a little "farming" to supply our own needs and sell to our friends.

Keith bought an old bungalow in town. That's all he did with his profits. Except give most of it to anyone with their hand out. And spend the rest at secondhand stores. You should go to his house sometime. The whole thing is crammed floor-to-ceiling with the old, used crap he collects. That's what he does with his time. He prowls around the Goodwill and antique stores when he isn't smoking weed and drinking beer and shooting hoops at the Rec Center with a bunch of old boozers. He's still sweet, though. He's a very sweet guy. He'll do anything for anybody.

Ah well, I hate it when people whine and moan about what could have been. There's nothing you can do about the past. No point wallowing in it. I just wish to hell I hadn't gotten that goddamn car home on time.

Twila Prevails

i. The coffee

PHONE BUZZES

Good morning, Wiggenworth and Wasp. This is Twila Tinsberry.... Tinsberry. Yes, it's my first day here. Well thank you ...
Yes, Mr. Wasp is in, but he is on another line. Would you care to
hold?... All right then, I'll put you on hold.

PHONE BUZZES

Good morning, John! Oh, you're off your line. You know you
have a call holding?... Oh, what can I do for you?... The coffee?
What about it, dear?... Well, no, I'm sure it hasn't been made if you
haven't made it, because I don't drink coffee. It disagrees with my
bladder!... Uh huh ... Oh! I see! You thought *I* was going to make
it. Well, let's just look that up, shall we? I don't think it was in my
job description. Let's see, I've got it right here ...

Yes, here we go: uh, billing, bookkeeping, typing, filing, appointments, phones, supplies, time management, keeping up the web-
site—no, there you go, it's not!... Well, yes, I sure can understand
that, John, but you know with a husband and four children—and
now six grandchildren!—why, I spend most of my time at home
in the kitchen fixing things for people, so naturally when I'm at
work I don't like to do it here, too. I'm sure you can understand

that, dear … Oh, I can *sympathize*—I'm the same way when I don't get to read my paper in the morning.

Well, you know what I think you need to do, John—I think you need to just go ahead and learn how to fix it…. It's *not* hard … I'd be happy to show you, too, but I'm just going lickety split on this report you said you had to have done by 11:00, and—say, you know your better bet would be to ask Mr. Massey at Massey CompuSystems across the hall to show you how. I saw him make it with my own eyes. Shall I give him a buzz?… Well, if you'd rather figure it out for yourself, there should be instructions on the side of the machine. Now, did you want me to put this call through to you yet?… Oh, you want to wait 'til you finish making your coffee—all right!

PRESSES BUTTON ON PHONE

Mr. Wasp will be tied up for about an hour, may I have him call you back? All right, will do. Bye.

CONTINUES TYPING

PHONE BUZZES

Yes, John … How do you get it to be stronger? Uh, put more coffee in, I suppose … Well, see, that will make it kinda weak if you don't put any coffee in … In that sliding container, I'm pretty sure. Yes, and then just pour the water through the screen, but be sure you have a pot under—Oh, are you *wet*?… All over your nice wool pants? Didn't get burned, did you? Thank goodness. You'd better soak that coffee stain in cold water right away, dear.

I beg your pardon?… Uh huh … Oh my goodness! Well no, I had no idea you felt that way!… You know, I thought it seemed just a little bit intimate when you called me "honey" on my first day here, but, well, I thought, gee, people have different views about office protocol. John likes to keep things very casual. I never dreamed that you would be offended if I called you "dear!"… Well, all *right* then. No "honeys" and no "dears."

I'm glad we've got that sorted out, John, because— … What about your name?… You know I thought you preferred being on a first name basis because, of course, right off you called me Twila, so naturally I just assumed!… Oh my goodness, I'm so…Well, certainly, if you would rather be called Mr. Wasp, I don't mind a bit if you call me Mrs. Tinsberry. Or, maybe, *Ms.* Tinsberry. Doesn't that have a professional ring to it? And, say, it might be a good idea to add my last name to that little name plate on my desk— … Oh, I won't keep you, if you want to put another pot on, go ahead … All right, see you later, dear—uh, John—uh Mr. Wasp. Oh gosh, it's easy to forget, isn't it?

ii. The seminar

PHONE BUZZES

Good morning, Wiggenworth and Wasp. This is Twila Tinsberry. May I help you?… Oh hi, Sandra…. No, I'm just having a sandwich at my desk. I was gone so long yesterday at that seminar that— … I didn't tell you about that? It was called Dress to Impress. Mr. Wiggenworth *paid* for me to go. It was a lot of fun. We had a buffet lunch provided for us at the top of the Hanover Building—real fancy!

PHONE BUZZES

Oh, I've got to go. Mr. Wiggenworth is buzzing me. Bye, dear.

Well, good morning, Mr. Wiggenworth. Say, I just want to thank you so much for sending me to that seminar yesterday…. Well, yes, I did learn a lot, and I met such nice people, too…. Just what you said—how to dress to look more professional. 'Course I didn't agree with some of it, but, oh, it was just real interesting…. Well, that they wanted you to wear these somber, conservative colors—your dark navy blues and blacks and grays, with maybe a mauve scarf to contrast— … Oh, *nothing* wrong with that, but, you know I got to thinking: this Dress to Impress idea, now is that why when you go out for lunch downtown here, you see this whole slew of business people coming out of their office buildings dressed all alike in these dark colors? It's quite a sight! Droves and droves of them. It kind of puts me in mind of this herd of Black Angus near where I grew up, coming down the hill on their way to the barn for their dinner.

Pardon me?

Well, I'd be happy to satisfy your curiosity, Mr. Wiggenworth, but I'm afraid you won't get a chance to see me dressed that way— … Well, 'cause, come to find out, you couldn't buy one of these Dress to Impress suits for less than $400!

They are?! Oh that's exciting. When are they coming?… Gosh,

we'd better get things slicked up around here if the Board of Directors is going to be here next week—

Take off for what?

Shopping for a suit?! Oh, no, I wouldn't want to take up work time for that! No, no. Now don't get me wrong, I like to look my best at all times, but, well, I'd be afraid of spilling copier toner on a $400 suit. No, I figure it's better to dress for a mess! Now did you notice this outfit I'm wearing today?… What'd you think of it?… Mr. Wiggenworth?

Yes it does, fits perfectly! Guess how much I paid for it? Oh, go on … No! Only $20.00 at the Goodwill. And it wears so well, and, I can just throw it in the washing machine and hang it up to dry. And then, too, I think our clients would rather talk to someone who's wearing nice bright colors.

What are *you* going to wear for the Board? Say, why don't you wear that lovely powder blue jacket with the palm trees on it, that one you were so proud of, that you got in Hawaii?… Yes, you did, you wore it to Mr. Wiggenworth Sr.'s retirement dinner. Remember he made such a cute joke about it?… Oh, I'm sure he didn't mean anything negative by it.… Well, if he did, that was just *his* opinion. You liked that jacket, and I thought it brought out the blue in your eyes so nice.

Oh, you did? Well, that was sweet of you. I'll bet the Goodwill was thrilled.

Pardon me?

No, no I'm sure about it. No, you can't buy Dress to Impress suits on a secretary's—er, excuse me, an Executive Assistant's salary.

A raise?! Oh, now I don't want you to think I was hinting, gosh no! Why, even if I *had* the salary for it, Mr Wiggenworth, I just think there's a whole lot of better things you can spend your money on than dressing to impress, don't you agree?… Oh. Well, if you've got a little extra money floating around, we can install that good set of waist-level filing cabinets we talked about. Then I wouldn't have to be stooping and bending all the time. What do you think?

No, I already checked it out, right around $400. Here, it says, "For the professional look … comes in black, gray, or navy blue with a cranberry accent." We could dress the *office* to impress! I can put the order in today and they'll have it installed before the Board gets here. …

Mr. Wiggenworth? You sound kind of glum. You're not worried about what to wear for the Board, are you? You'll think of something sharp, and, say, I've got this end covered—the annual report is done and all the accounting is in order—we're in ship shape.

Me? Oh, I think I'll wear my lime green suit with the lavender scarf to match the buttons. Won't that be cheerful?… Did that give you a chuckle? Good! And, say, thank you again for sending me to that seminar. I wouldn't have missed it for the world. Oh my goodness, where has the time gone? I'd best get on with my work. All right then. Bye now.

iii. The switch

PHONE BUZZES

Good morning, Wiggenworth and Wasp, this is Twila Tinsberry, may I help you? ... Oh, what a shame. Well, I'll tell him. Bye Bye.

PUNCHES PHONE BUTTON.

Mr. Wasp, they said they can't fix the air conditioning today. They're waiting for a part to come in.... You poor thing, you must be freezing! Out here it's just the opposite. Hot as blazes. Say, Mr. Wasp, why don't you just pick up your laptop and come and sit at my desk for a while. It's nice and warm out here. I'll trade with you, we're not expecting anybody.

Well, if somebody does come in, just send them back to me.

Mr. Wasp, with your terrible sinuses you should not be sitting in that cold while I'm out here just burning up. I'm coming right in.

TINSBERRY AND WASP TRADE OFFICES

Nice and cool in here! Bet this carpet is soft. Nobody to see me if I slip off my shoes. Mm, that feels good!

PHONE BUZZES

Yes, Mr. Wasp.... Oh, I'm afraid that chair is too old to adjust. Now if you want it lower, get rid of the extra cushion. I've got it there on account of the chair being so hard. 'Course you'd want it *higher*, wouldn't you? I'm afraid you're out of luck. By the way, I sure do like your view! Makes you feel like you're up in an eagle's nest, doesn't it?

Hmm?

Oh, is that fluorescent lighting a bit harsh? Well, I find that, too, but there's no space for a lamp on my desk.

Okay. Bye.

I just love this adjustable chair!

PUSHES PHONE BUTTON

Say, Mr. Wasp, I forgot to bring those financial performance ratios in here with me, could you just open up my second drawer and read me the numbers on the top of that sheet—and be careful that you don't bark your knee when you—Oh, did that *hurt*? That's annoying, isn't it? I must do that 20 times a week. Well, never mind, I'll get them later. And, say, you wanted two copies of that balance sheet, didn't you? It's right there by your elbow. Why don't you just pop it in the copy machine—

Oh, there's nothing to it. Just put in your number of copies that you want—in this case, one—and push the button that says "darker" and position the paper, I'd say right square in the middle and then set it for legal size and you're all set.

Machine's not *working*?... Well, did you push the START button, Mr. Wasp?

There you go! Good for you!

Pardon me? Which file did you want? ... Willamette? It's in the top file drawer right next to my desk.

Yes, aren't they? Just as tight as they can be. Be careful not to strain your back.

Oh gosh, what happened, I can hardly hear you?

Got your *tie* caught! Yes, that thing'll snap shut all at once. Can you pull it open?

Pretty cramped back there, no leverage. I *know*! Those drawers are terribly heavy. Well, just take and put your back against the wall, get hold of the drawer, but be careful not to pull too fast—

Mr. Wasp, are you there?

Yes, it'll tip on you. Can you push it back up?

I'll come in and help you, let me just get my shoes on—

All right, if you think you can do it yourself, but Mr. Wasp, there's not a thing wrong with getting help when you're being squashed by a filing cabinet.

Oh, you've got it? Good!

Waist level filing cabinets? Good idea! That would be a heck of a lot easier. I'll look in my catalogue for prices. Last time I looked they were around $400.

Say, are you getting kind of cranky? I know just how you feel. I used to go through that a lot. 'Course for me it was due to the Change, but you know I've heard that men go through it, Mr. Wasp, right about your age, too. Now what *I* did when I got cranky at home—and I really recommend it—I took the telephone into the bathroom and I called up my friend Sandra—of course she was going through it, too, at the time—and I said, "Sandra, I've got a cranky alert" and she'd say, "Okay, let her rip!" and then I'd scream into the phone. And she'd say, "Feel better now, Twila?" and—

Yes, sometimes there *are* other reasons for being in a bad mood.... Sometimes work *can* get us down. But honestly, there's not a thing wrong if you *are* going through the Change. It's just a natural process—

Certainly, I'll see if he's in, hold on.

PRESSES PHONE BUTTONS.

Mr. Wiggenworth, Mr. Wasp would like to speak with you.... Okay, I'll put him through.

PRESSES PHONE BUTTON. PUTS PHONE BACK ON RECEIVER.

Oh, my goodness!

PICKS UP PHONE AND DIALS A NUMBER.

Sandra! Guess what! I think Mr. Wasp has a cranky alert in to Mr. Wiggenworth. Isn't that sweet?

Coping with the Regime

i. The grasshopper and the ants

THERE WAS once a large, very lazy grasshopper.

All spring, summer and fall he leaped about from one blade of grass to another and never did a lick of real work. Meanwhile a colony of tiny ants labored at the base of the tall grasses which bent under his weight.

The ants worked prodigiously day in and day out in ceaseless toil to get enough to eat and to maintain their colony and store up food for the winter. They were always exhausted.

The grasshopper disdained the ants, whom he dismissed as "losers." He had no use for losers. He considered himself to be a winner because he had inherited long hopping legs, which allowed him to travel great distances and jump to great heights, while the ants beneath him struggled and were often crushed by his tremendous weight whenever he leaped to the ground.

But the grasshopper was not satisfied with his life. He wanted recognition. The ants were too busy eking out a living to notice what a winner he was. So the grasshopper began to show off for the ants. "Hey," he yelled, in his raspy grasshopper voice, "Look up! Look at how big and green I am. See how I could crush you with a single bound? You couldn't do that, could you."

The weary ants looked up and had to admit they couldn't.

"Wouldn't you like to be as big as me and leap around and crush others if they got in your way?" he said. "Believe me, it's a lot of fun."

They thought maybe they would like to do that, but how could they? They were very small and too busy earning a living.

"Believe me," he said. "I know more about earning a living than any creature alive."

He had their attention now. They began to take time off from putting up food for the winter, in order to gather around and listen to the grasshopper. He said, "You know why you can't leap around like me and crush others when they get in your way? You know why you have to work so hard all the time and have no time for leaping?"

"Why?" they asked.

"Because you're losers," he said.

"What?! Losers!" they exclaimed, offended.

"No, I said you're … *winners* being held *down* by losers."

"Oh," they said. "*That's* what you meant. That's okay then. But, now, who are the losers who are holding us down?"

"You name it," he said. "Bees, butterflies, slugs—they're all invading your territory, taking what should be yours." The grasshopper was improvising. What he said didn't really make sense, but he was enjoying himself. "I just tell it like it is," he said.

"He tells it like it is," they repeated. That sounded good.

Winter was approaching, and now that he had their attention, the grasshopper was counting on the ants to store up food on his behalf. They would have to put in even more labor. "All you have to do is work together," he told them. "You're good at that. And don't take any backtalk from the bees, butterflies, slugs, etc. Show 'em who's boss. Take 'em down. A swarm of ants can strip a butterfly of wings, legs and antennae in two seconds flat."

"He tells it like it is," they said to each other.

When winter came, the ants found there was no food left for

themselves. Somehow the grasshopper had appropriated it all. However, while reminding them how a colony of angry ants could take down bees, butterflies, slugs, etc., he had failed to consider what they would do when they finally realized they had put their faith in a lazy, narcissistic, double-dealing grasshopper. They would start with the long, hopping legs. It would not be a pretty sight.

ii. Dotage

THE NORTH KOREAN dictator, Kim Jung Un, called Donald Trump a "dotard." Such a delightfully archaic word! Today no one would say someone is a dotard. We'd say the person has Alzheimer's Disease or senile dementia.

When you get to be seventy-three years old, as Donald Trump (and I) are now, and you walk across the room to get your reading glasses and have to retrace your steps to remember what you were going to get, that's when you ask yourself, "Am I a dotard?" Or maybe someone says, "What's your favorite movie?" and you say, "My absolute favorite is … Oh, what is the name of that movie? I loved that movie. It was the one starring … um … Oh, what's her name?" This is another occasion when you ask yourself, "Am I a dotard?"

Then you go for your annual physical, and you're given that MMSE test—that ten-minute, thirty point Mini Mental-State Examination. Any score under twenty-five is not good news. Your doctor says, "Your score is perfect! Thirty points. Your cognition is fine" and you feel very relieved for several weeks.

So this North Korean sociopathic megalomaniac dictator took it upon himself to diagnose the American sociopathic megalomaniac aspiring dictator without having seen the results of his Mini Mental-State Exam. Of course no one has seen the results because I'll bet you a million to one the President's doctor has never dared to give him the test despite what he claims.

But *is* the President a dotard? Does he exhibit any of those warning signs listed by the Alzheimer's Association? Like having problems finding the right word or calling things by the wrong name? Repeating himself? Showing poor judgment and decision making? Is he unable to manage a budget? Does he have trouble developing and following a plan? Does he become easily upset when he's out of his comfort zone?

I think he needs to take that MMSE.

And I know how to get him to do it and reveal his results.

We put together a group of, say, seven Republican state—not federal—senators, all of whom are privately alarmed at the impact the President's behavior is having on their chances for re-election. They come to Washington and propose to treat the President to dinner at a high end restaurant in order to express their appreciation for the great job he's doing. Of course he accepts that invitation.

Then, at dinner, the legislators start chuckling amongst themselves about a ten-minute test they've all taken.

"What test?" asks the President.

"The MMSE!" says the Arizona state Senator, suggestively. "Measurement of Men's Sexual Energy. It's a test of sexual prowess."

"Sexual … what?"

"Uh, *power*, Mr. President. Sexual power. It gives you a score."

"I should take that test," says the President. "Did I ever tell you that I'm so rich I can grab a woman's—"

"Yes, you did mention that once," interrupts the Colorado state Senator.

"Believe me," says the President, "that's sexual power."

"Mr. President, you'd never imagine that the items in this test have anything to do with sexual power, but studies have shown it's right on the money. George Clooney scored very high. Obviously, his sexual prowess is big."

"Believe me, I'd score biglier than Clooney or anyone else. Where can I get the test? I'll take it."

Several of the men pat their pockets pretending to look for copies. The Connecticut state Senator pulls out the test. "Oh great! I've got an extra copy here."

The Senator from Delaware administers the test to the President and scores it. The others squeeze in for a look at the results. "Whoa," they say. "*That* is one significant score. George Clooney didn't come anywhere near a score like that."

"You shouldn't be surprised," says the President, "have you seen my wife?"

Suddenly, the New Hampshire state Senator looks troubled. "You know," he says, "if the biased liberal media get hold of this score, they'll just say you're lying about it."

The President nods.

"Well," says the Senator from Nevada, "then we should all be official witnesses to it."

He takes the pen, and just below the score he writes, "We avow and confirm that the President of the United States, Donald J. Trump, took this MMSE test; that the test was administered according to the protocol; and the score of twenty accurately reflects the President's performance."

The legislators and then the President all sign and date the document. The New York state Senator puts it in the inside pocket of his suitcoat for safe keeping. The President of the United States takes out his phone, holds it in both hands, and raises his thumbs.

iii. The toad spell

"YOU CAN READ it as plain as day in the entrails of this pig." The others lean forward for a look. A lustrous sheen glazes the viscera. "If this continues without intervention," the diviner goes on, prodding a lobe of liver with a stick, "the Earth will be desolated. Do you see here?" Her audience of crones tut and tsk, sigh and mutter and shake their heads sadly to see the coasts drowned, the verdant woodlands become desert, life in the sea and on land uninhabitable.

"So, my Sisters," says the fortune-telling witch, looking around the circle, "how do we respond to this crisis?"

Remedies, potions, spells, and incantations recall themselves to the minds of the aged practitioners during the several minutes of silence that befalls them.

Before long the eldest of the witches—eight hundred years, if a day—supporting herself on her broom, rises from the giant tortoise shell upon which she sits, and casts her rheum-clouded gaze around the group. "You may call it vulgar and indecorous," says she, "but I propose the old-fashioned recourse of turning the offenders into toads," upon which pronouncement she eases herself down again onto her amphibious hassock and smiles a toothless smile.

Her proposal evokes a good round of laughter, in which the elder herself participates, but when the hilarity has subsided, a pause ensues, suggesting to the group that their sister has hit upon an agreeable solution.

The Toad Spell. Uncouth, out-of-date, over-used, but in simplicity and parsimoniousness not to be matched. No complicated, drawn-out series of incantations prone to mistakes in pitch and stress and tiresomely repeated until gotten right. No potions, the ingredients of which must be collected from the four winds and the ends of the Earth under successive new moons, starless nights, etc. etc. etc. Yes, the Toad Spell by comparison is a mere snap of the fingers.

"Recall, however," warns one of the assemblage, "that we have *forsworn* the practice of turning people into toads."

The prognosticating witch looks thoughtful. "So we did. But many years ago, Sister. Centuries, in fact."

"Has it been so long? How time does fly!"

"Surely, given the urgency of the situation, we may reconsider the decision."

"Was there a reason for forswearing the practice?" interjects the youngest of the group.

"Yes, and it was this: that the ease of administering the Toad Spell led to the temptation of abusing it in moments of temper."

"That is true," replies another. "But we have all of us matured since then. We have learned to separate motives of vengeance from those of necessity."

They look around at themselves and consider their years complacently, for even the youngest, a comparative toddler, is over two hundred years old.

"It would be in defense of humanity," says the fortune-teller, bringing them back to the point, "that we should consider applying the Toad Spell. There are leaders—plutocrats and their minions—who could bring the Earth back from the brink of extinction if they chose, but who are resolved to ignore the emergency in order to cling to personal wealth and power. They are assisted in this by the support of dogmatic theocrats not unlike the Salem, so-called, Fathers, if you remember that fiasco."

"You are suggesting we turn those people into toads?" again ventures the toddler humbly. "All of them? Would not the Earth be rather plagued with toads in that case?"

"It already is, in a manner of speaking," replies the soothsaying witch.

Peering around the circle through her ancient spectacles the eldest crone inquires, "Are we of one mind then? Toads? Or some other remedy?"

"Toads!" goes up the unanimous cry.

"Then toads it shall be."

Giving a diffident little laugh to concede her lesser experience, the toddler among them asks, "Do we turn them into toads at once then, or wait in hopes the perpetrators will vindicate themselves before it is too late?"

The eldest puts the question to the fortune-teller: "Is there reason to doubt the course these plutocrats and their minions will pursue?"

"None whatsoever," says the seer, after another quick scan of the prophetic guts.

"At once, then, I say!" There is a hint of glee in the old crone's voice. "*If* we are in accord."

In accord they are. The malefactors are parceled out, a great many to each sister.

And so the assembled sorcerers ceremoniously take their places, each closing her eyes to keep clearly in mind her first designated victim. In deference to her seniority, the octocentenarian is accorded the privilege of transforming three of the more egregious villains.

Now, at the eldest's signal, the crones utter the simple incantation which will initiate the spell:

Hark to this enchanting ode,

Seek out the ones on lofty roads,

Or gilded rooms of rich abodes,

And change them all to cringing toads.

All that remains to rid the world of its worst offenders is a collective snap of the fingers. To this end, the sisters raise their hands and press thumbs to third digits. In a sprightly manner, the eldest snaps hers, once … twice … thrice.

In a flag-draped room of the White House, an obdurate, unruffled Press Secretary is fielding questions from a large crowd of vociferous media representatives. Her responses—"I do assure you I will certainly work to make sure I get that answer to you." … "I gave you the best information that I had at the time." … "Actually, I'm interpreting what the President said. I'm not reversing it.". … "You guys need to take a step back." … "The President was joking."—have not, so far, been illuminating.

Suddenly, she disappears from the podium. The journalists assume she has dropped her notes and bent down to pick them up. When, after some seconds, she fails to reappear, the few reporters with favored status take the liberty of approaching the podium, concerned that she might, finally, have passed out from the daily exhaustion of defending so many lies on the fly.

Others in the press corps wonder if there is a trap door behind the podium with a tunnel leading toward the Oval Office. When, upon investigation, there is no apparent egress to a secret chamber and still no sign of her anywhere, the members of the media scratch their heads and type their various dispatches, all of which have the same gist: *Press Secretary Leaves White House*. Meanwhile, a small toad tries to disentangle itself after accidentally hopping into the folds of the national flag, which has, unconscionably, been allowed to sag close to the floor.

* * *

While passing through his native state of Indiana, a renowned theocrat, who is also the first man in line for the Presidency, visits the Evangelical church of which he was once a long-standing member. The minister's sermon today is from Exodus, 8: 1–14 regarding the plague of frogs visited upon the Pharaoh's lands and how Pharaoh duplicitously promised Moses he would let the Israelites go if the plague were lifted, whereupon God killed the frogs, who "*were gathered together upon heaps, and the land stank*."

Following the sermon, the honored visitor is asked to lead a prayer. Solemnly, he walks up the steps to the altar, his nicely trimmed white hair giving him a distinguished look.

Suddenly, before the entire congregation, he is transformed into what appears to be a frog. As he hops up and down the carpeted steps, the people are thrown into confusion. Is this a Divine message? Is this frog the harbinger of a larger plague of frogs that the Deity plans to visit on their *church*?

His wife, having a Master's degree in Science Education, exclaims, "He is not a frog! He's a toad!" No one is quite sure if there's much relevance to the distinction. She runs forward, scoops up the toad and holds it protectively to her bosom as if it were a pet rabbit.

* * *

A breathtakingly under-qualified president is alone in his penthouse on the 58th floor of his hotel in New York City. He is seldom at this apartment, but he's killing time before a meeting he doesn't want the press to know about.

While he waits, he multi-tasks—exercising his thumbs on a smart phone, watching the Fox channel's repeat coverage of his latest campaign rally, and eating a cheese burger. When he is finished with all that, he practices his putting on his golf simulator.

He seldom thinks of looking out the floor-to-ceiling windows that predominate in the apartment, or of opening one of the gilded casements to let in fresh air. Not being interested in natural phenomena, he doesn't pay attention to birds passing or the sun setting or clouds billowing. A large black crow flies toward the window and seems to look in, but he doesn't notice it.

While he is golfing, he thinks about the buttocks of the new housekeeper who started work yesterday and speculates on the likelihood that her immigration status will make her vulnerable to persuasion, and keep her silent afterwards.

Just as he misses an easy putt, the apartment and everything in it loom up enormous around him and he finds himself on his belly against the extremely deep and bumpy pile of the carpet (though he doesn't realize that's what it is) and covered by something like an orange blanket, lined with a wide mesh.

At this moment, the housekeeper, thinking he has already left for a meeting, lets herself in to clean. Mistaking the orange object on the rug for an outsized pair of flashy underpants, she picks it up gingerly between thumb and forefinger and gets quite a fright to find a brown toad dangling by one foot caught in the mesh underneath.

"*Mierda!*" she cries, throws open a window and tosses the whole thing out. It's a very long way down. Fortunately, no one is standing underneath. In fact, no one even *hears* the splat.

Diplomacy

T HE PRESIDENT slides into bed. He lies on his back with his eyes open.

"Still can't sleep, Barack?" His wife gently rubs his chest. "Been walking the halls?"

"How long can a person go on this way? I'll be hallucinating pretty soon."

She caresses his cheek. "You did sleep a little, earlier. You were snoring for a while."

"Sorry if it kept you awake."

"It used to, but now the sound is soothing."

The President sighs heavily.

"My thoughts loop around all night—minutiae, life-and-death decisions, it doesn't matter. I stew about some little gaffe I made with the Press. I imagine the consequences if we fail at the environmental summit."

Thick curtains have shut out the light of the moon. He turns to his wife.

"I've got nothing left in me. And I have to be up for that 6:00 A.M. flight to Brussels."

"Can you sleep on the plane?"

"It'll be nonstop work and briefings. Do I call him *Sir*? *Prime Minister*? *Mr.* Prime Minister? *Your Excellency*? Shake his hand?

Bow? No one seems to know. Oh, and some staffer asked his aide if he wanted to vet our choice of translator. Translator! The man got all his advanced education at Oxford. His English is better than mine."

"Oh dear."

"You can bet that piece of information went straight to the top. So before we even start talks, he's insulted. It took me a year to get this meeting in a neutral location."

"You've still got a couple of hours before you go. How about hot milk?"

The President shakes his head in the dark.

They meet in the Grand Hall of Brussels' Royal Palace. The ornate entrance is wide enough to preclude one head-of-state having to enter behind the other. They have an hour alone before their entourages join them and the formal talks begin. At one end of the large room, a gilt Louis Quatorze table has been laid with a silver carafe, two small cups, and a platter of pastries. Heavily brocaded divans have been set end-to-end, at an angle to each other.

The President offers his hand. The Prime Minister shakes it briefly, his face drawn and severe, the eyelids held sardonically at half-mast. The men sit down and ask perfunctory questions about their families.

"Your daughters study languages in their American schools?" the Prime Minister asks pointedly.

"French, Chinese, and Arabic."

There is a silence. The President lifts the carafe and raises his eyebrows at the dictator, who picks up a little cup and holds it out. The President pours. "Turkish coffee is very strong," he says.

"And yet, it is ineffectual at keeping one alert." The man's voice is hoarse and sounds tired.

The President notices for the first time the watery redness of the dictator's eyes, the dark circles beneath them.

"Uh … Mr. Prime Minister …" The President hesitates. He runs his fingers over the silk upholstery of the divan and presses them lightly into the cushion. He looks up at the dictator's eyes. "Mr. Prime Minister," he begins again, "why don't we take a nap?"

The dictator stares. Then, very slightly, his mouth twitches upward and his cheeks soften.

The President presses buttons on his digital watch alarm. "Forty-eight minutes?" The dictator glances at his vintage gold Rolex and nods.

The two men bend down and unlace their shoes. They curl up on their divans, the tops of their heads only inches apart. Their snoring does nothing to disturb each other's sleep.

The Diaper Standoff

Kathy to Mom: Friday, April 5th, 7:13 P.M.

—Hi, Mom.

—Hi, Kathy. Oh, you shouldn't be spending money on a long distance call.

—I'm on a plan, Mom, remember? Unlimited calls.

—Well that's good.

—Are you resting?

—Oh, some. But you know your dad. He wants his meals on time.

—*Mom*, you need to rest after surgery!

—I know. I'm resting.

—How is Dad?

—Pretty much the same. Except now he's upset about the bills for the operation.

—You *needed* that surgery, Mom.

—If it doesn't work, your Dad'll be fit to be tied.

—Did the doctor say what the chances are?

—He said some percentage. Sixty percent? Or eighty percent?

—It'll be a relief not to wear that protective underwear anymore, won't it?

Kathy to Sherry: Saturday, April 6th, 7:00 P.M.

—Hi Sherry. Is Mom having any more problems with leaking?

—Well, she went through a couple of disposables this afternoon.

—That doesn't sound good.

—But she thinks the improvement isn't supposed to start right away.

—How's Larry?

—Oh, he was over there today, fixing the fence around the pasture. But, Kath, wouldn't you know Dad got on him for getting the wrong barbed wire.

—What was wrong with it?

—Nothing. Just something for Dad to criticize him about. Will you guys be flying out here for Mothers' Day?

—Yes. Can you and Larry manage things till then?

—Yeah.

—I just wish I didn't live so far away, Sherry. I feel guilty leaving you two with all the responsibility.

—Oh, Kath, it's expensive to fly, and you were here for a whole week for her surgery.

—Well, it's an hour round trip drive for you, Sherry, plus being on your own with the kids.

—Bob has them every other weekend. And I can sometimes get away during the week. Don't worry about me.

—I'm just glad Larry lives so close.

Sherry to Mom: Monday, April 8th, 8:15 P.M.

—How often are you having to change the pads, Mom?

—I've had to use a new diaper every two and a half, three hours or so.

—Is that any better than before the surgery?

—I can't really remember, Sherry. Maybe it was every hour and a half or two hours before?

Kathy to Mom: Friday, April 12, 7:18 P.M.

—How are things, Mom?

—Oh, Kathy, your brother's kind of upset with me.

—Why?

—I've got so many of these used diapers piling up. Sherry gets them for me in 18-packs from Kmart. I don't know what to do with the used ones, so I've been putting them in garbage bags and setting them in the shed. They put off a pretty bad smell after a while. I asked Larry to take them to the landfill, but he won't.

—Why not?

—Oh, he says the diapers don't break down. They're not ... what's it ... uh ... biodegradable?

—Yes, biodegradable.

—He bought a big package of cloth diapers and he wants me to use them and wash them out and use them over. I guess he's right about it, but ...

—Mom, you're too sick to mess with all that.

—Well, I do feel kind of tired, and with your dad laid up, I don't know if I can manage it.

—Do you want me to talk to Larry about this cloth diaper business?

—Oh, I don't want to make a fuss.

—Hi, Kath.

—How are things going, Larry?

—Okay, I guess. I was over at the house last weekend. Worked on the pasture fence.

—How's Mom? Do you think that surgery helped her?

—Doesn't seem like it. She's put another bag of those diapers in the shed. They don't break down, you know. I got her some cloth diapers pretty cheap. You can get them in a pack of twenty, and then you can wash them out and reuse them.

—Who's going to do that, though, Larry?

—Well, I think Mom can do it. She's been doing the laundry for her and Dad.

—Larry, you've got to wash them in *very* hot water, even use bleach, to keep them sanitary. That can't be good for the environment either.

—You wouldn't have to use bleach. You could use vinegar. And hang them on the line in the sun.

—She doesn't have the strength to carry a laundry basket full of wet cotton diapers up the stairs and out to the clothesline and do all that bending and stooping, and Sherry can't be there all the time.

—Well, I could help her.

—And how's she going to carry four or five soggy diapers around when someone takes her into town to eat or shop? She'll hardly go anywhere now, as it is. She would just stop going out at all, and she needs a break from Dad.

—I know, but I wouldn't feel right about hauling them to the landfill. They'll sit there for the next thousand years.

Sherry to Kathy: Sunday, April 14th, 4:07 P.M.

—Well, Kath, we've got a crisis.

—The diapers?

—Yes, I've been bringing her the disposable ones, and usually Larry will carry their trash out to the landfill, but he won't touch this.

—Yeah, I heard.

—So there's this great big smelly pile of diapers in garbage bags sitting out in the shed, and more going in every day.

—She's not getting any better?

—Doesn't seem like it.

—Poor Mom.

—I could drive the thirty miles over there and back and haul them away myself every week but it needs to happen more often, and Larry is only five miles down the road.

—Well, he's got a point about the environment, Sherry, but there are times when you just have to make exceptions.

—That's what I told him.

—What does Dad say?

—Oh, he's oblivious, as far as I know. Mom doesn't want the subject to come up with him.

—Is Larry still pressuring Mom about wearing the cloth diapers?

—Well, kind of. She doesn't like to go against him. He does so much around the farm for them.

—I'll talk to him, Sherry. I was going to call him today anyway.

Kathy to Larry: Sunday, April 14th, 4:47 P.M.

—Did you get things sorted out about the fencing, Larry?

—No, I still can't find the damned barbed wire he wants. I can't go running all over the state trying to find something that doesn't exist anymore. I'm putting in sixteen-hour days on my own place. Now he's all over me because the Co-op won't take back the barbed wire I unrolled.

—Does he ever thank you for going to so much trouble?

—Hell would freeze over.

—How's Mom?

—That surgery didn't help her at all. She's still going through diapers like you wouldn't believe.

—Have you figured out what to do with them?

—Did you know that ninety percent of what goes in the landfills in this country is so-called disposable diapers? And none of that is recyclable, Kathy.

—Yeah, that's a bad thing. But you know, Larry, Mom isn't really in a position right now to do any extra work. She's pretty weak.

—I just can't see myself throwing four or five bags a week full of dioxins, sodium polyacrylate, and TBT in that landfill.

Kathy to Dad: Sunday, April 14th, 6:41 p.m.

—Yeah?

—Dad! You're answering the phone!

—Mildred's off somewhere.

—How are you doing?

—I'd be a whole lot better if your brother would get off his butt and get that damn fence fixed. He picked up the wrong barbed wire and put up fifty yards of it before I could stop him. I'd do it myself if I could get around better.

—How's your hip?

—So so.

—How about the swelling in your legs?

—It's there. Why do you need to know about it?

—Just wondering. Where's Mom?

—Probably upstairs in the bathroom. Mildred! Phone!

—That's okay, Dad. Don't interrupt her.

—Mildred! Come out of there and pick up the phone!

Mom to Kathy: Sunday, April 14th, 6:43 P.M.

—Is that Kathy?

—Hi Mom. How are you?

—I don't know what to do. I don't think that surgery helped a bit.

—Oh, I'm so sorry, Mom. What does the doctor say about it?

—I left a message with his office last week but I haven't heard back.

—Let me or Sherry call him for you.

—No. I don't want him to get mad at me for bugging him too much. Then I won't get any help from him at all.

—You're not getting any help *now*. I'll call, Mom.

—Well, if you think you have time.

—I have time.

—Doris called, wanting to bring me out to that new buffet for your cousin's birthday. But I don't know …

—Oh, you should go, Mom.

Kathy to Sherry: Friday, April 19th, 8:11 P.M.

—Sherry, what's the latest on the diapers?

—Larry just will not take those diapers to the landfill. Even if

Dad was willing to do it, he couldn't drive off the property, with his eyesight and his bad hip.

—Larry is going to have to be the one to haul those bags away.

Sherry to Larry: Friday, April 19nd, 8:37 P.M.

—Hi Larry. I'm sorry I can't get down there this weekend. Bob has the flu, and he can't take the kids. They've got a bunch of sports events I'll need to drive them to. So. Did the situation with the fencing get sorted out?

—I just went ahead and put up the fence with the wire I'd already bought.

—Good for you!

—Dad was pissed off, but he wanted his fence up, so now it's up. He's so damned stubborn, he'll gripe about it for the rest of his life, but there was nothing else to be done.

—It's nice of you to do it. It's a lot of work. And what about taking the diapers to the landfill?

—I'm thinking about it, but I don't know.

Sherry to Mom: Monday, April 24, 6:04 P.M.

—What's the matter, Mom?

—I saw a rat in the shed. Oh, Sherry, if there's one thing I can't stand, it's a rat! It was running across those bags of diapers. I don't dare tell your dad. But I don't know where else to put the bags. I can't keep them in the basement. I have a lot of trouble going up and down those steep stairs. And I wouldn't want to draw rats to the basement, anyway. I just don't know what to do.

Kathy to Sherry: Friday, April 26, 7:32 P.M.

—Sherry, where is she putting the diapers since she saw the rat?
—I think she's putting them on the porch for now, but it won't be long before some raccoon or dog comes along and rips them open.
—Something has to be done! She says she's using eight or ten diapers a day.
—I'm going over there this weekend, Kath, but I kind of hate to put those bags in my trunk with that smell, and Larry's so stubborn, he'd never let me take his truck for that purpose.
—What's the story with that worthless doctor? Could he care less?
—I can't get ahold of him to find out.

Kathy to Mom: Sunday, April 28th, 4:29 P.M.

—Can you tell me why you're crying, Mom? What's happening?
—I can't go anywhere. I'm so tired of being stuck in the house. I wanted to go to that buffet for your cousin's birthday last week. But I just couldn't, with all this leaking. It's my own fault, I guess.
—How is it your fault?
—I'm worse than a baby. At least with a baby you pretty well know when they're going to need changing. Your Dad's disgusted with me for all the time I spend in the bathroom.

Kathy to Sherry: Sunday, April 28th, 7:16 P.M.

—If only she would put her foot down! I would give my soul to see that—just once for her to stand up to Dad and Larry, both.
—If she would just tell Dad, You shut up about the bathroom,

and Larry, You get rid of those diapers *now*, however you have to do it.

—She's like a hostage.

—Yes, she is. Except you can negotiate the release of a hostage.

—Yeah, and a hostage would run if she saw the chance.

—She won't run, Kath. She never would. She never will.

—So it's still down to what to do with the diapers.

Kathy to Larry: Friday, May 3rd, 7:42 P.M.

—Hi, Larry. Any change in the diaper standoff?

—I pulled all that mess out of the shed along with the bags Mom has on the porch and took them to the landfill.

—You did?! Wow! Wonderful! What changed your mind?

—I just got sick of Dad hassling me.

—Dad? When did Dad get into the discussion?

—I don't know. This week I guess. He was bugging Mom about it.

Kathy to Mom: Friday, May 3rd, 8:16 P.M.

—So, Mom, I heard the problem has been solved about what to do with the diapers.

—Yes. Your brother's going to come every few days and take them to the landfill.

—How did that come about?

—Well, I told Larry that Dad wants him to throw them in our dump by the creek so we wouldn't have to pay the landfill fee.

—Dad wants him to do that? No kidding?

—Well, I don't know. I didn't ask him.

—Didn't ask Dad?

—Not really.

—Ah. … And Larry wouldn't want to risk polluting the creek.

—No, I don't guess he would.

—The landfill would be the lesser evil.

—I expect so.

—Well, that's good news. And how was your leaking today?

—I think … maybe a little better.

Kathy to Sherry: Friday, May 3rd, 8:48 P.M.

—Sherry. No need to call in the SWAT team. I gather that our mother has just negotiated her own release.

Prodigy

THE EDITOR *is working in her office. She lifts the phone and talks to her secretary.*

—Madeline, have you sent out those last three rejections I put on your desk?

—Not yet, *the secretary says.*

—Oh good. Would you please bring them back in? I'd like to handwrite a few lines before you send them.

—Lucy is here. Should I—

—Oh, she's here? *The editor glances at her watch.* Uh … yes, certainly. Bring her in.

After half a minute, the secretary ushers in a little girl, about eight years old.

—This is Lucy, *the secretary says. She lays the letters on the editor's wide desktop.* Lucy, this is Ms. Craft. She's the managing editor here.

The editor rises and comes around to shake the little girl's hand.

—I'm glad to meet you, Lucy.

—I'll just get on with my work, *the secretary says and goes back to the outer office, closing the door behind her.*

The little girl is wearing a straw hat with a wide red ribbon around the brim. She is carrying a brown accordion file and wears an oversized wristwatch with a red band. She says, "Thank you for taking the time to meet with me, Ma'am. I know you're very busy."

The editor smiles at the formulaic courtesy. These two lines must have been coached and well-rehearsed.

—Well, yes, *she says,* I am a little busy this morning, but I'm happy to take out fifteen minutes for a chat. *The girl glances at her watch.* Your mother has been a great helper to me. I don't know how I'd get through my workday without her. *The editor pulls a chair up to her desk and invites the girl to sit. Then she returns to her swivel chair. There is a momentary silence.*

—I like your hat, *she tells the girl.*

—Thank you. My grandma gave it to me.

—Do you enjoy wearing hats?

—I enjoy wearing this hat because it looks like the hat in "Children at the Beach" by Mary Cassatt.

—Oh, your grandmother is an art lover then?

—I don't think she is. But I am.

—So … you are … how old?

—Eight and a half.

—Eight and a half. Quite a big girl. What's your favorite class in school? Your mother says you like to write. Do you study writing in school?

—We won't study writing until 5th grade. My favorite class is art.

There's another silence. The editor is not used to talking much with children. The girl looks at her watch again.

—We have 13 minutes left. Will we have enough time to talk about my stories? *she says, her eyebrows tilting anxiously.*

—Of course. *The editor leans forward.* I see you've brought something with you. Would you like to put it on my desk so I can have a look?

The girl puts the file on the desk and extracts a thick stack of papers. The editor puts on her reading glasses and riffles through the pages, glancing at the titles.

—Well, you've written a *lot* of stories, haven't you? … "Lions of the Library," "The Green Checkbook Cover," "Where is Heaven?" "The Clubhouse Murders" ... The Clubhouse Murders! That sounds pretty grim. What's it about, can you tell me?

She lays the story down and assumes a receptive smile.

—It's about how these boys that belonged to a club collected all these different insects and butterflies and flowers and put them in jars and boxes and kept them in the clubhouse and looked at them and played with them until they died.

The editor straightens for a moment. Until the insects and flowers and things died? *The little girl nods. The editor squints as if she is remembering something. She leans forward again, resting her elbows on the desk.* Interesting subject *she says.* So. Your mother tells me that you'd like to write and publish books?

—Yes, Ma'am. And illustrate them, also.

—Oh yes, I think she mentioned that. When did you start writing?

—When I was two years old.

—Two! You knew your letters then? You could use a pencil?

—I used a keyboard.

—Goodness! I started using a keyboard when I was twenty. Of course, computers were rather new at that time. *She chuckles.* You've been writing for ... let me see ... over six years then. Your mother *claimed* you were a very advanced little girl. *The child shrugs.* So you write stories.

—And other things.

—What sorts of other things do you write?

—Here. *She pulls some pages from the back of the pile. The editor glances through them.*

—Poems.

—Yes, Ma'am.

—So you're a poet, too!

—Yes, I am.

—Do you have a favorite poet? Someone who inspires you?

—Edna St. Vincent Millay and Edgar Allen Poe. They're my favorites.

—And do your poems rhyme? *She picks up a page.* Oh, I see they do.

—Some of them do.

—Ah, *some* of them rhyme.

—The others are free verse poems. That means they don't have to rhyme.

—Thank you for explaining that to me.

—You're welcome.

—Let me see …

The editor reads aloud.

THE BEACH CREATURES
They come from underneath the beach
And poke up through the sand.
With squeals and sputterings they preach
And tentacles demand …

—This is a rhyming one, I see. Very nice. You must like beaches.

—Yes, I love beaches. The poem goes on.

—I see that it does … quite a few pages.

—Here's a shorter one. It doesn't rhyme.

—Well, let's have a look at that … *The editor reads aloud.*

"Deep down in the dismal dungeon of my desires—"

The editor looks up. She says, You seem to have acquired quite a grasp of alliteration …

She starts again.

"Deep down in the dismal dungeon of my desires
There lurks a vile, insidious thought.
It heaves its shackles against
the crumbling stones,
Wrenches them from their iron moorings,
Frees itself.

I hear it ascending the ancient stairs,
Oh no, disgusting hateful sentiment,
Stay imprisoned, reveal not

My vengeful, ungenerous nature.

Too late. Too late. It has reached the door.
It blinks in sunlight, opens its treacherous mouth,
Pronounces in hoarse tones the thought I tried
So well to hide.
It speaks with my tongue.

—Well! *The editor is momentarily at a loss for words. She removes her glasses.* Well, my goodness! *She looks over the poem again and at last says,* The title is … "Green-Eyed Monster"?

—It's a satirical poem.

—Satirical. And what were you satirizing?

—I was satirizing myself.

—Yourself? So what exactly is the poem about?

—It's about jealousy.

—Jealousy. Of course.

—"Green-eyed Monster" is a way to say jealous person.

—Yes, that's true. I knew that, but I'd forgotten. And what prompted you to write about this subject?

—I was jealous one time.

—May I inquire of whom?

—Of whom I was jealous was my little brother.

—Hmm … And did someone give you some help with this poem?

—Yes.

—I thought that might be the case.

—My mother told me how to spell "ascending." My dictionary was all the way upstairs.

—Oh.

The child leans forward, her elbows on the desk. Do you think I should write a subtitle? I thought of "A poem in the manner of E. A. Poe" because it's also a parody. But would a subtitle be too explicit?

—Explicit?

—Wouldn't people feel their intelligence was insulted if the idea was spelled out like that?

—Ah. Maybe. So this is a satire of yourself *and* a parody of Poe in one poem.

—What they have in common is hyperbole. I wanted it to be funny. But, do you think it's funny?

—Yes … yes, I do. And I think you're correct to let the reader figure it out. *She stares at the girl for some seconds.* And so you hope to publish stories—

—And poems, too, I hope.

—And poems. Well, you certainly have a flair.

—Thank you. Do you want to see my illustrations?

She pulls out another sheaf of papers from the folder and hands them to the editor. At the bottom of each picture is written the title of a story or poem and "Plate" with a Roman numeral by it: I, II, III, and so forth. The editor lays them out and studies the pictures for some time. The little girl looks back and forth between the pictures and the editor's eyes.

—Are these the Beach Creatures?

—No, those are the boys in the clubhouse.

—They seem very … elongated. Have you been influenced by the painter El Greco?

—I'm … not sure. I was just watching the boys through a knothole in the shed at Grandma's house.

—Ah. Well, I guess that explains it … So you've illustrated every story and poem?

—Some of them have more than one illustration.

—So they do.

There is a long pause. The girl breaks it by asking,

—I haven't written a whole book yet. Can I publish stories? I guess they're too short. *She searches the editor's face.*

—Well … not necessarily. We usually gather stories or poems together into a longer collection.

—Does a collection have to be a certain number of pages? If you make it into a book, does the printing make the writing longer or shorter?

—I would say longer. You've used a very small font.

—Would I have to have editing on my writing?

—What did you have in mind by editing?

—Cutting them and pasting them and putting different parts on different pages and deciding the best fonts.

—Yes, you might want some editing.

—Would you show me what to do or would you do it for me?

The editor thinks for a moment.

—I'll tell you what. Why don't you leave your writings and drawings with me and give me time to study them and think exactly how much editing needs to be done … and other things. Then you can come back and we'll discuss it.

—When will we discuss it? Should I come tomorrow? I know we can't discuss it on Saturday because your office is not open on a week-end.

—I'll talk with your mother. We'll figure out a time.

The editor reaches out, shakes the little hand again, and rises, but the child stays seated.

—What would happen if you had a fire?

—A fire?

She nods.

—Oh, you mean here at the office?

—If *we* had a fire I wouldn't worry because I could bring my folder with me when I ran out of the apartment.

—Ah! I see the problem. You don't have copies?

—Yes, I have copies, but these are the original ones. *She lowers her eyes.* I thought … maybe someday they might be valuable.

The editor stares at the pile of papers.

—I can imagine they might be. *She taps her chin, thinking.* How about this? I'll put your manuscripts in the safe. It's fireproof.

She goes to a safe in the wall and spins the dials. The child follows her and watches intently.

—If a fire comes, and the whole room burns down, the safe won't burn?

—Exactly. That's why they call it a safe.

—That's good.

The girl returns to the desk and stacks the pages, jiggling the stray sheets into place. It takes her quite a while to make the stack orderly. When she is done, she puts them back in the folder and holds it up. The editor takes it, gently slides it among other folders in the safe and closes the door.

—Is it locked?

The editor spins the dial.

—It is now. *Patting the girl's shoulder, she smiles down at her.* Let's get your mother and go out to lunch.

The girl looks at her watch.

—But I don't have any time left, do I? The fifteen minutes is over.

—So it is. But we have to eat, don't we.

The little girl gets up and skips to the door. The editor follows her and takes her hand. As they walk out into the reception area, the child looks back over her shoulder and glances solemnly at the locked safe. The editor nods to the child's mother.

—Madeline, will you join Lucy and me for lunch? I think we should discuss a niche for her work, don't you? A specialized audience it would be suited to. Maybe you have some ideas. *The mother, smiling, rises from her chair behind the reception desk, sets the phone for voicemail, and follows them to the elevator.*

—"Niche" *the little girl says.* "'Niche.' I like the 'shhh' at the end. It sounds like whispering."

Fragrance

O N THAT FIRST day of class, I raised my hand and said to the TA, "Excuse me, I don't want to inconvenience anyone, but I wonder if I could ask the other students not to wear perfume or cologne to this class. I'm allergic, and fragrances make me dizzy and give me headaches."

"Well—" the TA began, uncertainly.

A guy in the front row interrupted her, "You can't let her tell people what to wear or not wear. She can't force us to go by her rules—all that politically correct crap. There are other people in this class besides one Stalinist, hypochondriac, nutcase."

He reeked of Old Spice. I'd sat down two rows away from him and I could still smell it. Even if you weren't allergic to perfume, it had to be nauseating. Nobody else said anything one way or the other. The TA fiddled with her laser pointer and looked at her syllabus for several seconds while we waited for a response.

"Well … let me check with my professor," she replied with that shifty lack of eye contact that said first-time teacher.

"Goddamn loony," the guy muttered.

"I believe it's supposed to be written on the syllabus that reasonable accommodations are made for people with disabilities," I said.

"Disabilities!" The guy snorted.

"Okay …" said the TA, casting a glance out the window, then

at the fire extinguisher by the door. "Maybe we could go ahead and start class, and, like I said, I'll check with my professor before Wednesday? Okay?"

I picked up my books and moved to a desk several more rows from the Old Spice man. Then I got up again and cracked a window open.

After class he squeezed in next to me in the doorway, pressing against my shoulder and transferring Old Spice fumes from his jacket to my hair. "You people are maniacs," he said.

I would be walking around all day now in a miasma of cologne until I could get home to wash. I was already starting to feel dizzy, and in half an hour I would come down with a migraine that would leave me two choices: spend the next three days in bed with a cold pack wrapped around my screaming skull or stumble blindly through classes with the equivalent of steak knives lodged in each eye.

He shouldered his way past me. "Fucking Femi-Nazis," he said.

All at once, like the pre-seizure vision of an epileptic or the epiphanal illumination of a saint on the rack, the truth visited me. I was a Nazi, a nutcase, a Stalinist, a maniac. What action was denied me? What was there that I could not do?

I staggered after the man, and halfway down the hall grabbed him by the neck of his jacket. He swung around, and I took hold of the fragrance-soaked fabric of his sturdy denim lapels.

"Listen, you stinking cesspit, if you come to class wearing Old Spice again, I'll have you shot."

He tried to pull away, but I clutched his jacket tighter. I wasn't feeling too steady on my feet, and the more in his face I got, the dizzier the fumes made me, and I thought, If I go down, you're going down with me. Then he broke and ran. He dropped his notebook on the way and didn't stop to pick it up. I've actually had no trouble with him since.

Allure

God, I hate Ashworth. Too many little kids. What time is it? 3:00! We missed the best sun. Grandview Pool is better. At least there's grass to lie on. But what's the point? No one goes there. How about this suit? Beyond cool, don't you think? White's good. Yellow sucks. Last year I had a yellow suit. What a barfbag. I think I look pretty sexy in this one, though. Except for my neck and my collar bones. And my nonexistent boobs. And my stomach and my calves and my feet. But everything else looks great.

You want to do me first and then I'll do you? SPF 25! God, Jen, that's *way* too high. Does your mother pack your lunch, too? I don't want to be here for like two hours and still be a ghost. Here, I've got 15. No, forget it. I'm gonna lie on my back first. I can do my *own* front, thank you. This stuff smells like crap. You want some? Okay, whatever.

Oh god, these pathetic boobs are like disappearing across my chest when I lie on my back in this suit. The only way I don't look like a complete pre-pube is if I prop myself up on my elbows and squeeze my tits together. Hand me those towels, will you? I gotta make cushions or my elbows are gonna *fuse* to this concrete.

These disgusting collar bones. Sexy? Oh sure. Like Barney Fife's daughter. Who is Barney Fife? On "The Andy Griffith Show"? Don't you watch the classics channel? Never mind. See? If I prop myself up, my collar bones look like tray handles, but if I don't, I've got zero cleavage. Like how? Oh, I'll try it. Hmm. It *helps*, but if I press my chest forward like that, doesn't that give me a pencil neck? Yes it does. I can feel it. Gwyneth Paltrow! Yeah right. *Ostrich*, you mean. I gotta tuck my chin in to camouflage this gross giraffe neck.

Oh god, there's Jamie. Hide me, Jen. I don't want him to see me yet. I'm such a ghoul. I gotta get like really hot so my cheeks'll have some color. I wish to god someone would make blusher that doesn't wash off when you sweat. They do? *Now* you tell me, you brat. Where do you get it? Does it cost like a million dollars? Twelve? That's not *too* bad if my mother wouldn't be so disgusting about making me pay for my own makeup. She's such a hippy.

Oh barf, look at my hipbones. If they stick out any farther, they'll break through and make my zombiehood official. Believe me, I'd be *ecstatic* if I could take some of yours. The thing I do is stick my stomach out and keep it that way so I don't look like a total famine victim. I just have to breathe up in my chest.

How long have we been laying here? Only five minutes? Tell me when it's been ten minutes. I gotta cross my legs the other way every ten minutes or I'll get one tan leg and one white leg. No, side-by-side doesn't work. If I don't cross them, my calves look like sticks. When I stack one on top of the other, it kind of spreads out the muscle on the top one. Stand up and look down on them. Oh don't be a jerk, just do it. So don't they look shapelier this way? See? I told you. And you gotta flatten out your feet, you know, if you want them to tan right. Because your toes *shade* them, Einstein. You get one of those nerdy tennis tans like you were wearing little anklets, which make *my* calves look even skinnier.

Where's Jamie now? Don't be obvious! You see him? He *left*? Oh great. I told you we should have come earlier. Who's still here? Jacob and Ryan? I guess that's better than nothing. *Now* what time is it? Two more minutes. Do you see my sunglasses? No, forget it.

The only thing I've got going for me is my eyes. Thank you. The last thing I want to do is cover them up. People are always going, "Do you wear like tinted contacts?" And I *don't*! But who's gonna see my eyes if I'm wearing goddamn sunglasses. I used to wear them and take them off when I saw someone coming over, but it's too hard to keep taking them off and putting them on while I'm trying to squeeze a little cleavage. God that sun's bright. No, I *can't*! If I turn away from it I won't get any color on my face.

It is so fucking hot. Are you going in the water already? Just spritz off, it's easier. Why couldn't I have *your* hair? It looks great when it gets wet. When *I* come out of the water I look like George Washington. My hair is like pasted to my head and my forehead looks huge. Look. This is not a forehead, this is a *five*head! Plus, if I mousse my hair when it's wet, it dries flat. Or else I have to stay in that scummy dressing room and hold my hair under the hair dryer for a hundred hours. That's how long it takes my goddamn hair to dry, it's so fucking *porous*! I'm just gonna stay here and spritz.

Hey, you know what? I just noticed. If you look straight ahead—not up, or down at the water, but if you look at something dark like that tree trunk on the other side of the pool? You can keep your eyes pretty wide open even without sunglasses and they don't water too much. Try it. See?

Okay, go on. I'll watch your stuff. No, I don't want to now. I'll come back with you on a weekday morning early when no one's around and maybe I'll swim with you then. Or, hey, Jen, let's go to Grandview on Monday. You want to? Come on! My Mom can drive us. Jamie doesn't usually go to Grandview, and he wouldn't be there on a weekday anyway 'cause of his job. There's shade there, and we can go in the water. It might be fun.

In the Mood

ON A MUGGY July evening, a young married couple prepares to go to bed. For the sake of spontaneity, she inserts her cervical cap well beforehand, as usual. They go into the kitchen for a cold drink before turning in.

She says, "God, it's hot!" He laces his fingers into her hair, lifting it off her neck, then goes to the sink, soaks a clean kitchen towel under the cold water tap, wrings it out and lays it on her neck. She thinks, How sweet. And this puts her in the mood.

He got in the mood moments earlier when he noticed beads of sweat trickling into her cleavage and soaking into the edge of her tank top. He wondered if she was too hot to feel like doing it, and brought her the cold towel. Now she stretches her tank top up in front, takes the cool cloth from the back of her neck and mops around her damp breasts.

In the next moment, the tank top is around her waist and the two of them are on the floor. Oblivious to table legs and cabinet corners, they grapple each others' clothes off and roll across the linoleum, naked flesh squeaking. He turns onto his back to let her straddle him. With eyes closed she rises up on her knees, impetuously reaches inside to pull her cap out, and flings it across the room.

She sinks onto him again, and for a moment they're suspended like that: she, with an ecstatic smile on her lips, her face raised toward the ceiling, he with his hands clutching her breasts, his mouth open. Then she falls forward onto one hand, takes his penis with the other and starts to guide it in, but even as her fingers embrace it, the purposeful vector of a moment before is getting soft and directionless, a spongy bit of sea vegetable, sliding out of her grasp.

Frogwise, she crouches down on him, her knees on either side of his hips, and kisses his jawbone. He lays an arm across her back, but except for the silent rise and fall of his rib cage, he lies inert as a felled tree, the sweat glistening like dew in his chest hairs.

She strokes him a little more, but nothing is happening below. Above, a great deal is going on. What?! she's thinking. He doesn't want a baby after all? Instantly the correlation between the cap's ejection and collapse of the erection has taken place in her mind.

He's thinking, What? She wants to start a baby *tonight*? This is disturbing, but he hasn't quite pinned down why.

So. What were all those conversations about then? she asks herself, excerpting silently from the most recent of them: "*The mountains would be a good place to raise kids.*" (Last *month* he said this.) "*I really look forward to doing a better job than my own dad did.*" (Just two *weeks* ago.) She stops stroking.

He's a step behind her. The motive for her action is still hazy, but he's starting to piece together clues. Does she think I don't *want* to have kids? After all our conversations?

"Honey," she says, "are you out of the mood?"

"Yeah."

"Is there a reason?"

"It was the interruption, I guess."

"Oh. I'm sorry."

Sorry, hell, he thinks.

"Are you sure it's that?"

"I just *said* it was." And he turns away.

As soon as these words are out of his mouth, what's bothering him comes into focus. I get no *say* in this decision? he asks himself indignantly. What the hell! Does she think I don't want to have kids and she has to *trick* me into it when I'm too turned on to protest?

She is struck by a lightning twinge of guilt—How could I have interrupted such a delicious moment? What was I thinking?!—but anger rumbles close behind. Wait a minute! Interruptions happen—the phone rings, the cat jumps on the bed. Once I forgot to put in my cap. There was plenty of endurance *then.* He even helped me put it in.

His mind wanders onto the subject of feminism. *"It's my body, so it's my decision"* is that what this is about? Great way to enter into fatherhood, without any say in the matter. He notices his teeth are grinding. He consciously relaxes his jaw.

She starts remembering things, all those declarations he made before they got married. What were they, lies? *"You'd be a good mother, you're so easy-going"* (Three weeks after the first date.) *"We'd be great parents together, we complement each other"* (Two months before the wedding.) What *was* all that, a ploy? In an unconscious, habitual gesture, she presses her lips together and juts out her jaw.

I've *told* her I want kids. So what's the problem? If she's ready now, why doesn't she just ask—*"Honey, what do you think about making a baby tonight?"* What's this decision by fiat when she's got me on the brink of coming? Does she think my brains are in my dick?

Her mind is clicking away now. Maybe that was his strategy for getting me to marry him. Keeps his fingers crossed behind his back while he agrees to have kids. But why? She remembers how competitive he is. Maybe he said all those things just to beat out the competition. He once told her she was a prize. At the time it had seemed like a compliment.

He disengages his arm and clasps his hands behind his head; her cheek rolls into his armpit. She pushes herself off him and lies on her back with her fingers laced over her belly. They are silent. After some minutes of lying side by side like two bas reliefs on a tomb, she says, "This floor is getting hard," and gets up. A half hour later he follows her to bed. Eventually they sleep.

The next morning is crisp and blue, not so muggy. Happy chirping finches anticipate the alarm clock. He kisses her goodbye when they leave for work, and she reconsiders her conclusion of the night before. Maybe I was wrong, she thinks. Maybe it was just the interruption after all.

So that evening in the bathroom when she has taken out her contact lenses and he's brushing his teeth, she decides to test the waters.

She strips naked, steps into the red thong bikini that never fails to arouse him, and stands where she's reflected in the mirror. She sees him see her. He gets that half smile on his face. Ordinarily, now—or just before this—she would insert the cap in front of him. Instead, she backs toward the door, saying, "No interruptions this time, honey."

She goes to the bedroom and lies down on her back in bed with the sheet around her bare feet and her thighs a hand's width apart, but when he climbs into bed a few minutes later, he turns on his side away from her. "It's a lot cooler tonight," he says, and pulls the sheet over them. She says "Yeah," and turns on her side too, curling into herself. Eventually they sleep.

For the next three weeks she continues to conspicuously not put the cap in, but for a different reason now. Why should I mess with it if he isn't interested? she mutters to herself, and worries about staying married to someone who doesn't want children.

This is no good, he thinks, several times a day. How can I have kids with a woman who has to be this much in control? The expressions *feminine wiles* and *emasculation* glide like piranhas in and out of his mind.

Then it dawns on her that she ought to have had a period two weeks ago. She feels different. Something in her body is changing. A cancellation comes up and she gets in to see the gynecologist that same afternoon. The test is positive.

"Pre-ejaculate can contain small amounts of sperm," the doctor tells her.

"But only a little bit got smeared on me. How could that work its way in?" she asks, gripping the arm of the chair.

"It probably took a ride on your finger when you pulled out that cap, and it decided to hop off and keep going."

"But what about the spermicide in there? How could it survive the spermicide?"

"Well, it's not common, but it can happen."

He isn't home when she gets back. She fixes herself an iced tea and drinks it while she paces the kitchen, her thoughts ping ponging. Could I bring myself to have an abortion? But why should I have to? I don't *want* an abortion. But what if he leaves? Could I raise a child by myself? Is it fair to have a child without a father?

She needs time to think. But then he's home, friendly in the detached way he's adopted for the last three weeks. He comments on how hot it's gotten again, asks her a few questions about her day, which she answers untruthfully, and for a moment he looks at her, *really* looks at her, she thinks, as if he sees something different. Does he guess? He must have noticed the missing period. But she forces a smile, which he returns without his eyes participating—a smile colder than no smile at all—and looks away. He gets a beer from the refrigerator and withdraws to the porch to read a Tom Clancy thriller but before escaping into the distractions of Cold War espionage, he thinks, She doesn't give a damn about me.

In the kitchen she pours herself another iced tea and focuses her thoughts on how to keep him from figuring out the news of her pregnancy until she can settle on her own attitude toward it and propose a course of action. As she crushes an ice cube between two molars and plays the pieces with her tongue, an idea for buying time occurs to her.

That night before bed she joins him in the bathroom. As if nothing has gone on in the intervening weeks, she puts in the cap, making sure he can see her in the mirror. Then she goes into the bedroom, leaving him to finish brushing his teeth.

He stands holding the toothbrush in midair, dumbfounded. This is the perfect apology, he thinks. No words, no re-hashing. She just puts the thing in: *"You're right. I was wrong."* He sets his toothbrush down and looks at himself in the mirror, pleased by the definition of his pectorals. He's been working out a lot more the last three weeks.

Suddenly he's very much in the mood. He spits out the tooth-paste, washes his mouth quickly and hurries into the bedroom where she's lying on her side under the sheet. He climbs in and draws close to her, sliding an arm under her neck.

When she feels the hard-on pressing against her back, she gets a little shock, forgetting for a moment all that's passed, or not passed, between them since the steamy evening on the kitchen floor. Tentatively, she places her hand over his other hand, which has crept between her legs. She breathes a sigh, which he takes as a signal to proceed.

Though his enthusiasm is urgent and rising exponentially, he moves at a slow pace, having enough good sense, he tells himself, to be gracious about her apology. She is lying quite still. In the past she has shown him very specifically how to stimulate her, and now, having heard her sigh, he assures himself she is zoned in on his caresses.

A thought occurs to her: Now—when he thinks I can't get pregnant—now he gets turned on. His caresses irritate her and she rolls on to her stomach to get away from them. He takes this as an offering to make love from behind, his favorite position. This is generous of her! he thinks, and he's grateful, in love again, wanting to give. He whispers, "No, honey, let's do it *your* way," and rolls her over so she's on top.

This makes her literally sit up and take notice. Straddling him, she sees that his eyes are half-open and liquid in the dark, gazing on her with artless lust. Well, she thinks, he may not want to have children, but he does love me. And she bends down to kiss him. He rises up to her, holds her tight, groaning.

Without a thought in his head, loving her totally, triumphantly, he rises up with her, and on an impulse he reaches inside her with his index finger, manages to gently draw the cap out, and flips it on to the floor, where it lands with a plop.

For a moment they're frozen like that, he with his hard abdominal muscles pressed into her thighs, she on her haunches, head still thrown back. So! she thinks. Fatherhood wasn't the problem after all. It was about control.

And just as she realizes what the problem *was* and wonders why he couldn't have just said, "Oh, you want to make a baby? I think we should wait a little longer" or, "Okay, let's do it now," and just as she recognizes this as the kind of struggle they've always had and probably always would have, he drives deep into her once, twice, three times with gusto, and she lets him do it because he can't get her any more pregnant than she already is. She's so far from having a climax that she doesn't even consider faking one, but eases herself onto his chest and takes the opportunity of his being spent to lie there quietly and have a good and hard think about the future.

Junior Year Abroad

I F I HAD IT to do over again I would not spend a weekend in an unheated Oxford dorm room under a blanket in the dead of winter with a homosexual boy who says my legs feel rubbery in tights against his bare skin. And I wouldn't attend a student jazz session and stand without moving for three hours and forty-five minutes until the soles of my feet burn because I want to appear so enraptured by music that no one would guess I am ashamed of being unnoticed in my acetate mini-dress.

And when a young man, almost rid of an accent that marks him as the first in his family to attend university, pronounces on a soft afternoon in May that one does not stroll barefoot in the Queen's Botanical Gardens, I would continue to dangle a sandal from each hand, whether it embarrasses him or not.

If I had it to do again, I would again visit the British Museum, but many more times than once, and not only to look at the mummies.

I would still eat Cornish pasties, but just on the first few days, and only for lunch.

I wouldn't care particularly that my hair flattens and my bangs separate in the sooty air.

And I would not develop a lame knee when it comes time to look for an apartment and stay holed up in a cheap hotel room until my money runs out and have to be shown by the hotel clerk how to use the classifieds and finally hobble off to find a studio flat with kitchenette and shared bath in the home of a family needing extra rent and be greeted the next day, while struggling to bring in my enormous steamer trunk, with a question delivered in the received tones of Queen Elizabeth by the three-year-old child of the house: "Are you going on holiday?" and find that my knee is suddenly functional. On second thought, maybe I would go through all that again.

I would certainly go to Stonehenge again at dawn on a Sunday, but not with a pimply freshman who's borrowed his parents' Mini for the occasion and can hardly wait until Monday's classes so he can casually let it slip that he went to the country with an American bird two years older and claim that she put out in the back seat.

The second time around I would visit Stonehenge with my angel mother, if she had not lost her ability to distinguish Druidic slabs from Calvinist chapels, or a plane ride to England from a trip to hell. So I would probably have to go to Stonehenge alone. This time I would not find a twenty-five-hundred-year-old monolith spray-painted with a ten-foot peace symbol.

I might not stay in London at all if I had it to do again but would go immediately to the Lake District. I wouldn't hitchhike, though, and be almost abducted by a lorry driver and driven down a dead-end road through a forest and roughly propositioned and have to jump from the cab and run back down the road to the highway and be rescued by an old woman in a Bentley with a shawl over her knees, who would scold me for taking risks. This time I'd take the train.

But when I got to the Lake District I would—yes, I would again —stay in an empty castle-turned-youth-hostel and wake up in the morning shivering and be locked out for the day in a cold, drenching rain, and after trudging for miles along open road, chance upon a country tea room with a crackling fire in the fireplace and a view through bay windows of small dark ponies dotting the windswept hills. And there, in the tearoom, I would again spend the afternoon with a fellow traveler—met by chance—at one of the chintz-covered tables, where we would warm ourselves and grow euphoric on cups and cups of constantly replenished strong tea from a fat china teapot kept hot by a quilted tea cozy, and we would consume baskets full of scones with honey, and bowls full of sugar lumps, and pitchers full of cream (all free for the price of the first cup), and after a while—dry and warm—we would pull paperback mysteries from our backpacks, and by the waning afternoon light and the fire's glow, savor the fact that in a good mystery you don't know until the end how everything is going to turn out.

Satan Tweaks the Good News

THE LAST BOOK of the Christian New Testament, *Revelation*, predicts God's visitation of horrific plagues upon the world followed by a thousand years of peace, after which Satan, Satan's angels and earthly minions will unite to battle God for control of heaven and Earth. Ultimately, all people living and dead who believed Jesus to be a divine savior will rise to heaven while unbelievers, Satan, and his minions are plunged into hell for eternity.

Revelation is so full of symbolism, metaphors, and similes that Bible scholars through the centuries have made quite a decent living delving into the Old and New Testaments, poring over every image, every article and preposition to prove their fellow scholars have gotten *Revelation* all wrong.

It is little known that an irrefutable explanation of *Revelation* has existed since the time of the book's genesis. You may read it here.

***

Satan: Minion!

Minion: Sire?

S: Get in here. I need you to take some notes. What's the year?

M: 4.5 billion, Your Ruthlessness, or 95 C.E.—Common Era—or ... 95 A.D, depending on your point of view.

S: Ah, how the eons slip away. All right, take out your quill and get this all down. We've got some serious brainstorming to do.

M: I'm ready, Sire.

S: These Jesus followers are planning to put out a sequel to the old anthology. They're calling it *The New Testimony* or *New Testament*, something like that. They're going to patch together their so-called accounts of their man's life by impersonating that bunch who used to hang on his every word: "*Do unto others …*" "*Turn the other cheek …*" "*Love thy neighbor …*" "*Ye without sin cast the first stone …*" all that compassionate drivel.

M: But how can they claim to write as those disciples? Weren't those guys illiterate?

S: Of course they were illiterate. To say nothing of now being dead. But half the male population of Greece and Judea is named some version of John or Mark or Luke or Matthew. These new guys won't have to outright lie about who the authors are.

M: But Your Maliciousness, why are they going to the trouble?

S: Are you an imbecile? To bring in converts! In the future they'll call it marketing, or propaganda. It's my own invention.

M: I see.

S: I'll do the same as I did after those tribes inserted in that older testament the whole brutal chronology of genocides and land grabs committed by themselves and their enemies. Remember what I did?

M: Sneaked in the claim that it was God who commanded the atrocities? Portrayed him as jealous, wrathful and vengeful?

S: Yes, and, that if these humans didn't toe the line he would send pestilence, force people to eat the flesh of their sons and daughters, and so on and so forth.

M: Ew! I'd forgotten that part.

S: *Leviticus: 26:29.* A little over the top, but one of my better efforts.

M: They didn't find that hard to swallow?

S: Leave the puns to me.

M: Sorry.

S: You'd have *thought* that would have blown my cover, but no. If my idea of original sin hadn't blown it to start with, nothing would.

M: Oh, Sire, original sin was so …

S: Original?

M: Indeed.

S: And what about "*An eye for an eye and a tooth for a tooth*"? How did I come up with that? The cadence, the parallel construction. So elegant.

M: Right up there with "*Spare the rod and spoil the child.*"

S: Such alliteration! Think how many rage-aholic fanatics beat their children to death with that excuse. And … I can do it again by sabotaging their new literary effort. I'll compose stuff and slip it in when the scribes are overtired. Once again, they'll think it's the word of God.

M: I can't wait to read it.

S: Yes, I was meant to be a writer. But not a writer of these little aphorisms only. This time I'll insert something with more scope.

M: What did you have in mind, Your Scurrilousness?

S: Something mystical, poetic. Something terrifying, with abstruse symbols, puzzling metaphors and whatnot. Give it literary oomph. Maybe … a whole book of my own! A masterpiece. Yes! Make it the last book of their new anthology. How about this for a title: *Revelation*!

M: It has the ring of truth to it, Sire.

S: Doesn't it? And the beauty is, these Jesus followers believe that God inspires all their accounts. That's why this is so … what's the word …

M: Diabolical?

S: Exactly. If humans can believe old women are concubines of the devil because they prescribe chamomile for indigestion, what won't they believe?

M: Do they believe that?

S: They will, centuries from now.

M: God did create them gullible, Sire.

S: His mistake. And if you put something in writing, they'll automatically take it as … well, gospel. So. How's this for a plot for *Revelation*: God sics my avenging angels on the world, putting it through a meat grinder for a number of years—killing off a third of everyone and everything in the most hideous ways imaginable, then judges all the living and the dead on the basis of their devotion to him, the majority being hurled into a lake of fire and tortured for eternity while the paltry remainder look on from the clouds in glee.

M: Wow.

S: Yes, wow.

M: But ... uh—

S: Go ahead. We're brainstorming here. There are no bad ideas.

M: Well, Sire, just playing the deity's advocate, but … you only have to have a distant acquaintance with God to know that tormenting people and casting them into eternal torture by burning isn't really his way. Won't they get wise to the inconsistencies? You know— "God is loving, God is forgiving, God is merciful"—and all that?

S: You idiot, that's what they've *never* been able to get into their heads. Didn't you pay attention just now? Look how they sucked up those rapes, murders, and slavery I attributed to God's will in that first anthology. That book is full of holes you could ride a camel through. No, no. They simply justify utter inconsistencies with, "God works in mysterious ways," "No one can know the mind of God," blah blah.

M: Of course, Your Deviousness. You are wonderfully inventive if I may say so."

S: You may.

S: Minion! Get in here.

M: I'm at your service, Sire.

S: Here it is! The first draft of *Revelation*.

M: So fast! You're a marvel.

S: Yes, I am. Here's an excerpt. Listen to this: "*... and round about the throne were four beasts full of eyes before and behind. And the first beast was like a lion, and the second beast like a calf, and the third beast had a face as a man, and the fourth beast was like a flying eagle. And the four beasts had each of them six wings about him.*" Mystical, huh?

M: Excuse me, Sire, these beasts ... are they *our* beasts?

S: *His* beasts.

M: God's?

S: God's.

M: But aren't *we* supposed to be the ones with beasts? Serpents, dragons and so on?

S: Baffling, isn't it? And that's just one excerpt. Here. Read this part.

M: "*... I saw a beast rise up out of the sea, having seven heads and ten horns, and upon his horns ten crowns ... and the beast I saw was like unto a leopard, and his feet were as the feet of a bear, and his mouth as the mouth of a lion, and the dragon gave him his power ...*"

S: Great stuff, huh?

M: Another beast. So ... that's his beast, too?

S: Ours.

M: Ours? But ... "*crowns*?"

S: Counterintuitive, right? Read here.

M: "*And there appeared a great wonder in heaven; a woman clothed with the sun and the moon under her feet, and upon her head a crown of twelve stars*"—Our crown or his crown?

S: Just keep reading.

M: Sorry. "*And she being with child cried, travailing in birth, and pained to be delivered. And there appeared another wonder in heaven; and behold a great red dragon, having seven heads and ten horns and seven crowns upon his heads*" ... More crowns. ... Uh, forgive me, Your Treacherousness, it's probably just my ignorance, but ... it seems ... incomprehensible—er ... that is ... I mean to say, complex.

S: It *is* incomprehensible. It's gobbledygook. That's the beauty of it. They'll go nuts trying to interpret the "symbols."

M: So you want the reader to be confused?

S: Confused and overawed, as in "Say, I can't make heads or tails of this. It must be profound!"

M: Oh, yes. I see!

S: So. Take the manuscript away and come back when you've read it. I need a second opinion before it goes to print.

M: I'd be honored, Sire.

***

S: It took you long enough. Have you read it from beginning to end?

M: Yes, Your Heinousness.

S: And?

M: Well ... um ... all these numbers, Sire. The book is just twelve pages long and there are one hundred and two references to numbers of things or lengths of time or specific dimensions—seven trumpets, seven years of tribulation, seven candlesticks, ten thousand times ten thousand and thousands and thousands of angels; one hundred and forty-four people of tribes (twelve thousand of Juda, twelve thousand of Reuben, etc.); preparation of one hour and one day and one month and one year to slay one third part of men; three woes; sixteen hundred furlongs of blood on the ground; three unclean spirits like frogs—

S: You counted them *all*?

M: Well, I'm a little compulsive.

S: And did you find anything to tie these statistics together?

M: Uh, actually, no. But I would have had to study them longer!

S: Exactly. Jesus followers will study those numbers for centuries and never agree on what they represent.

M: What *do* they represent?

S: Nothing. I pulled them out of a hat. You can interpret them however you want, like Rorschachs. Get these people to go digging back to references that I stuck into the old anthology and insist they were prophetic—Hold it! That gives me an idea. I could shove some more so-called "prophetic" bits into their books of the new anthology, too. I wonder what their time frame is for getting those done? Hmm.

M: What are Rorschachs?

S: Not invented yet.

M: Oh ... Uh, Your Ominousness, I know you mean *Revelation* to be confusing, but I was just wondering—purely out of curiosity—if all these horses of different colors had any actual significance.

S: What, those four horsemen? Who doesn't like horses in a story? White, red, black, pale, etc. Say, maybe I'll throw in some carrots or apples ... No, maybe not. Spoil the drama.

M: There's a white horse as well as a pale horse. The pale horse—do you mean another white one?

S: Could be. I picture it kind of grayish.

M: And a rider on a white horse comes back later with a sword in his mouth. That's the messiah-type character, right?

S: Right.

M: So why does he come in earlier with the red horse and the black horse and the pale horse riders?

S: He doesn't. All four of those are angels.

M: Oh.

S: They bring five months of earthquakes, bloody hail, locusts, scorpions, oceans full of dead fish, etc.

M: You have angels doing that? God's angels or our angels?

S: God's.

M: And … five months?

S: You think it should be longer?

M: Oh, it's not for me to—

S: I thought five months was a nice inexplicably odd number.

M: Of course.

S: So. Ya like it?

M: It's certainly grandiloquent, Sire, but—

S: Did you like that foreshadowing toward the beginning, *"Blessed is he that readeth, and they that hear the words of this prophecy, and keep those things which are written therein: for the time is at hand?"*

M: *"The time is at hand."* It certainly encourages one to turn the page.

S: That was the idea. So what did you think of the sequence?

M: Was there a sequence? I couldn't seem to—

S: I scattered in a lot of sequence phrases: *"after these things …" "and when …" "and then …"*, but half the events are happening simultaneously or in the opposite order suggested.

M: So artful!

S: The second coming of this messiah character, for example. I imply he's coming soon and then he won't come. That'll have every little Christian sect for the next two thousand years incessantly bickering about it, claiming that "soon" means "in the distant future" or "now" or "sometime."

M: Delightfully illogical.

S: *I* thought so. And somewhere in all this will be a thousand years of felicity and peace. But will the messiah come *before* the thousand years of felicity and peace? *After* the thousand years of felicity and peace? The factions who claim to have figured this out will call themselves millenialists, pre-millenialists, post-millenialists.

M: So sly, Your Vileness. I prostrate myself before you. But … I hesitate to even mention this part: "*… Hold on the dragon, that old serpent, which is the Devil, and Satan, and bound him a thousand years, and cast him into the bottomless pit and shut him up.*" It refers to … *you*, Sire?

S: Yep. Keep reading.

M: Uh … "*… first resurrection …* etc. etc. *… Satan … loosed out of his prison, go out and deceive the nations—*" That part is very nice, but: "*… the devil that deceived them was cast into the lake of fire and brimstone, where the beast and the false prophet are, and shall be tormented day and night for ever and ever.*" Yikes.

S: Vivid, eh?

M: But doesn't it make you look like … well … a loser?

S: It does indeed.

M: Sire! I've never known you to be … dare I say … humble?

S: That's because I never am and never will be.

M: Then why—

S: Because anyone reading this would never guess *I* wrote it.

M: So …

S: So they'll believe it comes straight from God.

M: And the purpose would be …?

S: Ah. The purpose. Okay, now listen closely. Go back to my third chapter.

M: Third chapter. Got it.

S: Read Verse ten.

M: "*Because thou hast kept the word of my patience, I also will keep thee from the house of temptation, which shall come upon all the world, to try them that dwell upon the earth.*" The "I"—is that God you've got talking?

S: Yep.

M: Hmm.

S: I see I need to unpack it for you.

M: I'm afraid so, Sire. I don't have your subtlety of mind.

S: It's very simple: *Because you've waited patiently, believing in my word*—Clear enough for you?

M: As a bell, Sire.

S: *I'll keep you*—that is, faithful humans—*from being tempted*—"tried" (by me, Satan, of course). So far so good?

M: The "I" here is God again?

S: Obviously. Ergo, everybody on Earth but the faithful will end up suckers for sin. And eventually, centuries later, even though none of my inserted prophecies will have come true, a number of Jesus followers will mull those words over and come to an interesting conclusion. Try to follow me now.

M: I'll do my best.

S: Remember how I got them constantly massacring each other in the name of God?

M: Yes.

S: Now I'm going to get them to decimate the whole *planet*!

M: The whole planet? Astounding.

S: I'll wait until humans get so populous and so greedy that they'll think a floating island of trash the size of Texas is normal.

M: What is Texas, Sire?

S: A land mass in the future. Forget about it.

M: Sorry.

S: And when anyone suggests that countries should all get together in a coalition to reverse the trend, these Jesus worshippers will hold up *Revelation* and say, "World coalition? That's the Antichrist!"

M: The what? Where is that? I didn't get that in Verse ten.

S: Of course you didn't because it's only implied there. Now, look here in Chapter twenty, Verses seven and eight: "*And when the thousand years are expired,*" (Remember those thousand years of felicity and peace?) "*Satan shall be loosed out of his prison,*" (I get bound and imprisoned for a thousand years earlier in the story before I get dumped into the lake of fire) "*and shall go out to deceive the nations which are in the four quarters of the earth, Gog and Magog, to gather them together to battle: the number of whom is as the sand of the sea.*" "Deceive the nations." United *nations*. I'm surprised you didn't get it.

M: I'm afraid ... I still don't.

S: Uniting the nations is an antichrist thing to do.

M: Is antichrist you, Your Invidiousness?

S: No, it's bigwigs around the world who are in my pocket.

M: Oh. I expect there will be a lot of them.

S: Tons. And their fight against God will last seven years, or half of seven years—is that three and a half? Anyway, long enough to devastate the Earth in a cosmic battle at a nice central location ... hmm ... Des Moines? ... Tokyo? ... No. I've got it—Armageddon, down there by the Sea of Galilee. I'll plant the suggestion that God is suddenly, without warning, going to yank all the believers up in the air to safety in heaven and leave everybody else behind. Remember how in Chapter three, Verse ten he saved believers from being tempted? Everyone else will be ensnared by "*the nations*"— the antichrist—and then tortured forever for their disloyalty to God. People will call the yanking up to heaven "The Rapture."

M: "The Rapture."

S: Great catch phrase, don't you think? The *idea's* been around for ages, but I won't put the actual word "rapture" in *Revelation*. Instead, I'll put it in a series of twentieth and twenty-first century best-selling dystopian Christian thrillers with a flawed superhero. People will swallow it like cough syrup laced with codeine. Misguided preachers, ambitious right-wing politicians, they'll take it up and—bingo—a household word—and with such a ring to it.

Who wouldn't want to believe in … The *Rapture*!" Doesn't it sound like a bodice ripper?

M: *I* would read it.

S: And *then* when the Earth is an uninhabitable desert, imagine their faces when they meet their maker and he says "*Why*? Why didn't you cherish and protect my greatest work?" And they say, "To show our *faith*! To show our worship of *You*, Lord!" And he says, "But why didn't you have faith in my interventions? I sent scientists, I sent polar bears, I sent Rachel Carson and Al Gore. What part of Save the Planet did you not understand?" "But," they'll protest, "you wrote in *Revelation* that before the New Heaven and New Earth arrive, You will devastate the old Earth to punish—" "I did nothing of the kind. I never wrote that book." "Lord, you *must* have. It's so poetic, so mystical, so …"

M: Prophetic?

S: Precisely. And think about *this* … God might get so furious he'll hand these people over to *me*.

M: Really? Of course I wouldn't contradict you, Sire, but, you know God—despite your portrayal of him in that old testament—he's not really wrathful or vengeful.

S: His weakness, certainly. So. Now do you see?

M: Your Heartlessness, *Revelation* will be your *pièce de resistance*. I only wish you could get the credit for it.

S: Use the brains I gave you. That would defeat the purpose, wouldn't it! I will, of course, go by a pseudonym. I'll say the book was penned by … John, inspired by an angel.

M: Who is John? John who?

S: *I* don't know. Just *John*. John of Ephesus, John of Patmos. Name's been around for millennia. It's generic.

M: I am so ignorant. I abase myself before you.

Turning Mrs. Johnson

O
N THE BUS coming in to work that night Louise had stared out at the dark expanses of empty parking lots, sprawling discount stores and housing developments as city turned to suburb. The identical ranch houses, set in the middle of large plots marked off from each other by cubes of evergreen shrubs, looked as orderly and fussed over as a cemetery. The convalescent center blended in with these houses except that it claimed a full block, including the parking lot, and was lit by floodlights at strategic points on the snowy lawn.

Louise thought of her father's house, her younger sisters with years to go before they could escape it, her oldest brother enlisting and off to Vietnam at eighteen, the next brother maybe soon to do the same—anything to get out of there. She liked to think that in the morning the bus would drop her at the corner of the three-story brick building called Lorelei, just a few blocks south of downtown, where she would tuck herself into the Murphy bed of the one-room efficiency and fall asleep to the sound of the refrigerator switching on and off like a stroked cat.

She was only five feet two inches tall and a hundred pounds. At her size, she would never have gotten hired if she hadn't told so many stories about herself: She was a high school graduate. She had taken care of old people. She knew how to change beds and give enemas. She could turn paralyzed patients.

The hiring woman had glanced doubtfully at her height and her hair, which her sister had carefully plaited into cornrows the night before. Louise would be on probation, the woman said. If she proved she could handle the old people—clean them up when they soiled themselves, take blood pressures, and so on—the job would be hers. On the first night, Louise had been lucky; she had only to follow the older aide, Ardyce, and watch.

Ardyce was close to sixty. When they met, she'd shaken her head at Louise's small size and exclaimed, "How'd you get this job, anyways?" The answer, which Ardyce must have known, was that another night aide had quit without notice the week before, and the supervisor was in a pinch; Louise was the first person they had interviewed and almost everything she'd said about herself had been a lie, starting with her age, which she'd told them was nineteen.

Somehow, she had survived her first shift without being let go. She tried to memorize everything Ardyce did—sliding bedpans under heavy bottoms and sliding them out again without tipping them over, getting blood pressure cuffs around skinny arms and fat arms and pressing the stethoscope to the inside of their elbows. What Louise learned from these actions couldn't be discovered by watching, however, and she wondered what she would do when it came her turn to figure out the numbers that Ardyce had her write on the charts—160/87, 95/43.

Louise stood in the supply closet at the beginning of her second night and tried to remember what was supposed to go on the cart. On one wall, shelves were stacked to the ceiling with wash cloths, gowns, and sheets. On the others were soap, pitchers, paper cups, bent straws. She was pretty sure all of that would have been distributed already by the 3:00 to 11:00 shift.

But what about those fuzzy pads they called fleeces? Did they replace all the pads or only if they got soiled? She seemed to remember the fleeces lying underneath some kind of protector. She spied the box of blue plastic-backed rectangular sheets of paper—'chucks' or 'chux,' Ardyce had called them. She pulled out a stack of these and put them on the cart.

They would probably need more sheets and gowns and wash cloths and maybe talc if the ladies messed themselves. She tried to recall how many beds they had changed. There was the little skinny blind woman who thought she was in a hotel; the woman who blabbered all night at the top of her voice; the deaf old lady with cancer who had the sweet smile; the big paralyzed one—Mrs. Johnson. Louise had a moment of dread at the thought of the woman. Mrs. Johnson was rude and demanding. Louise would have to help turn her tonight. She might even be expected to do it by herself as a test.

When Louise finally pushed the cart into the hall, Ardyce was emerging from a patient's room. "What took you so long?" she complained and put her hands on her broad hips when she caught sight of the cart. "What'd you bring all them sheets for?"

"To change beds."

"Why so many?"

"Well, two for each bed?"

"What was you gonna do, strip everybody's clean sheets off three hours after they just got 'em on?"

"We got about five or six that *mess* the bed, don't we?"

Ardyce picked up a pillow case from the top of the pile and looked at it as if she'd never seen one before. "They mess, yeah, but not their *pillows*, not their whole *bed*! You *do* know which end *makes* the mess, don't you?" Louise didn't answer. "That's what we got chucks for, so we don't have to change everything. Parker and Cora's the only ones likely to mess up the whole kit 'n kaboodle." She made a chiding noise with her tongue. "We only need enough linens for them two plus draw sheets." Louise felt her face grow hot. She had forgotten about the folded draw sheets placed between the fleece and the chuck to move the patient back and forth across the bed so the dirty padding could be pulled out from underneath.

"Oh yeah," she said.

"I guess they don't use draw sheets where you did your 'private duty,'" said Ardyce. "Where was that, you said, 'Colorado'?" Her laugh ended in a cough that bubbled up from her lungs.

"That was a while back," said Louise. "I forgot."

Ardyce snorted. "You too young to *have* a while back."

They began their rounds.

Ardyce pushed the cart down the hall to Mrs. Parker's room and flicked on the light as they entered. The tiny emaciated woman was sitting bolt upright clutching the guard rails on either side of her bed with both hands.

"Is it time for breakfast?" she inquired cheerily as the two aides entered. "I don't believe I'm very hungry. Maybe just some tea and a biscuit."

"You know it's not no time for breakfast. It's the middle of the night." Ardyce chuckled. "Tea and biscuit!"

"Oh." Mrs. Parker favored them with a bright smile. "Well, I thought it was." Her wide open gray eyes were covered with a film as cloudy as dishwater. It was uncertain what, if anything, she could see.

Louise went around to the other side of the bed and gingerly pried the old woman's skeletal hand, finger by finger, from the steel rail.

"Come on now, Mrs. Parker," she said. "We gotta change you. Let go now."

Ardyce had already plucked the other hand loose and held it firmly in her own while releasing the bed rail. "You sure are slow," she remarked to Louise, as she rolled the old woman onto her side and untied her hospital gown.

Louise made no comment but stood aside as Ardyce deftly peeled the wet gown off Mrs. Parker and rolled the soggy bedding into a kind of sausage, pushing it in tight under the old woman's side. Ardyce worked so fast Louise could only look on.

"What you standing there for, girl?" said Ardyce. "Don't you see we need a new chuck and a draw sheet here?"

In her nervousness Louise couldn't remember how to fold the draw sheet. She picked one up and began putting the corners together. Ardyce watched, purse-lipped, foot tapping loudly on the tile. Louise's fingers fumbled and dropped the sheet twice to the floor before she got it folded.

Louise wondered how she was going to get through the night if this was how things would go from then on. Mrs. Parker was easy compared to some of the others, like Mrs. Johnson.

On Louise's first night of work, Mrs. Johnson's husky, sometimes breathless voice had begun to give orders as soon as Louise and Ardyce entered her room. Nothing they did had been quite enough or quite right, and there was a lot to do. A big swollen woman with small, shifty blue eyes, she was paralyzed from the shoulders down.

The most important job was turning her properly. Like moving a slab of concrete that had to be lifted, rolled and set down just so—that was what the operation had reminded Louise of as she stood uselessly watching.

This afternoon, after finally falling asleep, Louise had dreamed that Mrs. Johnson was floating like a blimp just outside the windows of her room. She caught glimpses of her through large tears in the shades.

"My, but it's chilly!" said Mrs. Parker wonderingly, her thin, naked body trying to curl up into itself for warmth. Louise held on to her hands while Ardyce wet a wash cloth and wiped the wrinkled bottom, leaving a path of gooseflesh.

While they worked, Mrs. Parker spoke companionably, as if addressing a husband across a dinner table. "I chanced to meet my neighbor, Mrs. Johnson, walking in the hall today and she remarked on the cold as well."

"If you seen Johnson walking, you seen a miracle," said Ardyce. "Johnson ain't been out of a wheelchair for five years."

"Perhaps you don't know the Mrs. Johnson I am referring to," replied Mrs. Parker. To Louise, she said, "Climb in bed with me, dear, and we'll talk."

Ardyce snorted. "Climb in bed with that smelly ass, you be crazy," she said under her breath. She tucked in a fresh sheet and a double layer of padding and rolled them up next to the dirty linen.

"Give her here," she ordered. She took the old woman by a shoulder and a hip and neatly rolled her over to the clean side. Ardyce was the kind of stout woman whose skin stretched smooth as canvas over hard muscles. "See, you do it fast, the patient don't suffer. Those ones with a lot of pain, you don't want to be pulling on 'em every which way. They ain't no rag doll. Joints hurts em. Float em over quick and easy like a log on water. Ain't that right, Parker?"

"That's right," Mrs. Parker replied, distractedly. She had caught hold of a filagree ring on Ardyce's little finger and was feeling it. "Well, that's lovely, isn't it?" she said.

"You like that? Husband give it to me thirty years ago, God rest his good soul." She turned to Louise, "Can you believe I could wear that on my ring finger once? Couldn't get it off with a crowbar now."

Mrs. Parker tapped Ardyce's swollen finger and said, "Keep it in your vault. I believe there are colored people on the staff."

Ardyce withdrew her hand.

"You *crazy*, woman." She nudged Louise. "Come on, girl. Let's finish up and get out of here before the colored people come in and robs the rings off our fingers."

Louise stripped the soiled bedding and dropped it in the hamper hanging from the cart. She helped to hoist the naked old woman upright again and hold her hands away from the bars while they slipped a new gown on her.

"That's better!" exclaimed Mrs. Parker. "My, but it was chilly. I don't know why it got so cold all of a sudden." Ardyce and Louise raised the bedrails and moved toward the door.

"Oh, wait a minute, please!" chirped the old woman in her bright sparrow voice. She was sitting very straight again, her face arranged in a gracious smile. "I've forgotten, does the hotel staff bring my breakfast automatically, or must I order it?" Ardyce gave Louise a knowing look.

"It comes automatically," said Louise. Ardyce laughed and shook her head.

As they moved toward the hall, the old woman unwrapped one hand from the bedrail and smoothed her gown. They heard her reply benevolently to the air, "Thank you so much."

Even before they reached Mrs. Johnson's end of the corridor, her calls were coming in a rhythmic drone: "Nurse … Nurse … Nurse … "

"Johnson wants over on her other side," said Ardyce. "Wisht she'd quit fussin' and go to sleep." Amen to that, thought Louise.

"Why don't you come when I call?" Mrs. Johnson said as they entered. She was lying on her left side, facing the door. Below the neck, she was dead weight. Only her reproachful eyes and her mouth were animated. She looked to Louise like a beached whale with a live Jonah peering out.

"You think we got nothin' else to do than turn you over every ten minutes?" Ardyce flipped the rail down and went around to the other side of the bed.

"My hip gets sore from the weight," Mrs. Johnson said.

"If you paralyzed, you don't feel no sore hip. How come you feel it?"

"I don't know. I just do. Come on. Turn me. And be careful of that arm." She groaned as Ardyce pulled her over onto her back and straightened her legs.

To Louise Ardyce said, "See, you don't want to be using your back on this one. You'll put it out for sure. You bend at your knees, like so. And don't be afraid to lay down on her, whatever you gotta do to get a hold on her and still protect your back. This way."

Now Ardyce lifted one of the heavy legs, shifted the catheter tube, lay the leg slightly bent on top of the other one, and grabbed the hip. Then she leaned in very close against Mrs. Johnson's chest and grasped her firmly under her shoulder as Louise looked on with her hands hanging foolishly out in the air in a feeble gesture of help.

"Go over to the other side and give her a push when I pull, but wait till I say."

Louise did as she was told, nervously fumbling at the catch to the rail so that it fell with a bang and shook the bed. Awkwardly, she put her hands on Mrs. Johnson's shoulder.

"One on the shoulder and one on the *hip*!" snapped Ardyce. "Use the sense God gave you. Now!" And before Louise had a chance to lean in for the push, she felt Mrs. Johnson's huge inert body turn slowly and smoothly away from her.

"My head is crooked! I can't breathe." Her voice was high and muffled. The side of her face had settled into the pillow. "Pull my chin out!"

Grumbling, Ardyce picked up her head and shifted it on the pillow. She stopped what she was doing for a moment and looked Louise up and down. "How old are you, anyways?"

"Nineteen."

"Nineteen! *Sixteen*, more like. When I started I was younger'n you. Didn't know nothin'. Just a skinny little thing like you, scared to death of them patients. I been doin' this for forty years. Okay now, watch," she said, "'cause next time *you're* gonna do it. They told me I'd have some *experienced* help here."

When Ardyce finished turning Mrs. Johnson, she stopped to take a few breaths. Louise listened guiltily to the rattle of Ardyce's congested lungs.

"No more bent than that!" cautioned Mrs. Johnson.

"Hush, I ain't done yet."

Ardyce finished the adjustments while Louise straightened up some clutter on the bed table. She felt momentarily relieved. The turning was over, at least for this round. Louise hoped she would find some excuse to avoid Mrs. Johnson's room on the next one; maybe another patient would ring a bell and she'd be needed somewhere else.

"That good enough?" Ardyce said to Mrs. Johnson. "It better be, 'cause we don't have the time to stand here all night moving you one inch this way, two inch that way."

"Yes, that's better, but now put the fleece between my ankles and take the blanket off my shoulders and put it under my arm." Louise pulled the cover down several inches. "No, no. *Under* my arm. I can't have my arm covered. I'll suffocate." They lifted the big lifeless tube of an arm and tucked the blanket under it. "Smooth it so there are no lumps." Her voice suddenly became ingratiating. "Please? If there's even a small lump, you know, I start to feel it."

She had the husky voice of a society lady from a film, Louise thought. She pictured her sometime in the past playing cards with other society ladies, sipping cocktails and smoking cigarettes like in the movies.

"Now just bring me a sip of water."

Louise held the glass close to her face, bent the corrugated straw and poked it into her mouth. The woman sucked on it, stopping several times to catch her breath. When she finished, Ardyce and Louise made a move to go.

"Oh wait," she said. "Put my clock on the other side where I can see it, and rub some Desitin on my hip where the red spot is."

"You want us to uncover you all over again just after we get through covering you up?" said Ardyce, shaking her head.

"I forgot about it before, but it has to be done. I don't want to get a bed sore." Ardyce pursed her lips and jerked the blankets down, but when she began to investigate the red spot on the hip, she became thoughtful and absorbed. She passed her hand several times back and forth over the spot, and patted it delicately. Mrs. Johnson's eyes strained in their sockets in a useless effort to look down her body at the exposed hip.

"Has it broken down yet?" she asked, tensely.

"Gimme some more light," said Ardyce to Louise, who switched on the overhead lamp. Ardyce pulled a pair of reading glasses from her smock pocket, put them on, and bent close to examine the spot. "Look here. See this? It's just red, not broke down. Feel that."

Louise touched the spot. "It's hot," she said.

"Sure it's hot 'cause she been layin' on it, but it ain't broke down like that one I showed you last night—that Miz Arnault." Louise remembered. Ardyce said, "Don't worry, Miz Johnson, You ain't got a bed sore here. Just a red spot, nothin' else. I'm rubbin' it for you." Her voice was unexpectedly reassuring as she massaged the hip for a minute or two. To Louise she said, "See, you got to keep an eye on them spots 'cause they can start to break down. Then they abscess on you. And you got trouble, 'cause how can they heal when the person can't get up and walk around, get some circulation to the area? Pretty soon you got a hole in 'em you could get your fist in. Here, you rub it some more while I check on Meyer—she won't need much." She dropped the dirty laundry in the hamper and pushed the cart out into the hall.

Louise tentatively drew her fingertips across the red spot and back again, not knowing whether to press lightly or deeply, feeling awkward and shy being suddenly alone with the big woman, and embarrassed by the expanse of bare hip under her fingers and the broad bare buttocks. She was glad Mrs. Johnson was faced away from her and couldn't see her or even feel what she was doing, since Louise thought she was doing it badly.

As if reading her mind, Mrs. Johnson said, "Rub in circles all around the spot. Use your thumbs to get a little pressure."

Louise massaged for a minute or so, silently, wondering whether she was expected to talk. She couldn't think of anything to say to the woman. It was a relief when at last she heard Ardyce in the hall coming out of Mrs. Meyers' room.

Mrs. Johnson heard her too, and said quickly, in a low voice, "Would you just check on me once or twice between rounds?"

"I don't know if I'm supposed to," Louise replied, uneasily. "I guess I can."

From the hall, Ardyce called, "Come on, we gotta finish up." Louise took her hand off Mrs. Johnson's hip, covered her again, and moved toward the door.

Mrs. Johnson stopped her. "Wait! Could you move my other arm out just a little bit?"

"Come on," said Ardyce, from the doorway. "We'll be here all night, 'Move this, move that.'" Louise moved the arm quickly and went into the corridor, turning off the light as she went.

"Leave the——"

"We know," said Ardyce. "'Leave the door open.' Please and thank you."

In the corridor they heard Mrs. Johnson cry out hoarsely, "Please, I think there's still a lump in the blanket." They moved on down the hall, leaving the door ajar, but just barely.

***

When Ardyce and Louise returned after rounds, the night nurse was at her station, leaning back in her chair and looking into the ward. She was a large white woman of about thirty-five with a teased bouffant hairdo ten years out of style. "Flynn's out of bed again," she said, shaking her head and chuckling. "That Flynn! Go see what she's up to."

Mrs. Flynn was in the only ward room. "Some new law says even a fancy private home like this one has to have one ward for poor folks," Ardyce had said.

Louise was glad to look in on Myrtle Flynn.

"There's nothing wrong with her," Ardyce had told Louise. "She's just a little dotty, got a bad heart and no family." The night before, Myrtle hadn't been asleep when they'd checked on her. She had been lying stretched out on her back—all six feet of her big-boned, ninety-eight year old frame. In Ardyce's flashlight, the huge droopy green eyes had shown white underneath like an old, sad-eyed cow. She gave the aides a broad, toothless smile.

"Hey, you gals better get to bed now or you'll be tired come morning. Who's that pretty little thing, Sis?" she said as they came closer. "Is that your youngest?"

"Sure thing, Myrtle," said Ardyce.

"Come here, sweetie, Auntie'll give you a fresh doughnut." Myrtle beckoned Louise with a plastic rosary she'd been holding against her chest. To Ardyce, she said, "Sis, we got to fatten up this pretty child," reaching out a big hand and closing it over Louise's small one.

Ardyce said, "Myrtle never wants nothing. Just see if she needs help to the bathroom," and she left to tend to another patient.

Myrtle declined the bathroom assist. "I can hold my water 'til morning," she said. "Better'n gettin' a spider bite on my fanny."

"It's an *indoor* toilet, Myrtle."

"Is it? Well, *there's* a wonder!"

When they had returned from the bathroom and Myrtle was back in bed, Louise stood looking down into her droopy-eyed smile for a minute until the eyes started to close and she felt the grip on her hand slacken. She laid the hand back down over the rosary on her chest.

That was last night; tonight when she entered the ward room, shadowy figures lay under sheets in three of the beds; the fourth bed was empty. In the center of the room stood Myrtle.

"It's late, Myrtle. Don't you think you ought to be in bed?" The old woman peered into the darkness.

"Why, what time is it?" she said.

"Two A.M."

"No! Is't that late?" Drawing her lips over toothless gums, she opened her broad mouth into a smile, sending a fan of creases across her great square cheekbones.

"*You* know it's late. Don't kid me," said Louise. Myrtle punched her and grinned. Louise held out an arm and was steering her toward her bed when the old woman stopped and took a step backward. "Myrtle, where are you going?"

"I mean to check up on my mama." Myrtle shuffled over to a bed in the corner where a small plump woman of about seventy was asleep flat on her back with her mouth open, blanket and sheet pushed down around her ankles. "Mama don't keep herself covered," Myrtle confided to Louise, as she bent to pull up the blankets.

"That's sweet of you to take care of her."

"Oh, psh!"

After she got Myrtle to bed, Louise wished she could stay there in the dark until morning.

* * *

Mary, the third aide, looked up from the lounge where she and Ardyce were eating their dinner and watching television.

"Miz Flynn up and about again?" said Mary. "You can*not* keep that woman down. Reminds me of my grandma. Got cataracts, she still tryin' to take care of everybody in sight, whether they need it or not."

Mary was tall and young, probably about twenty-five, Louise guessed. Because of her height, she could turn patients without help, so she did her rounds alone. Ardyce could have done hers alone too, but her swollen ankles bothered her and her heart wasn't good; she usually had to sit down at least once during rounds to catch her breath.

Mary turned the TV down. "Feel settled in now, Louise?"

"I'm starting to get their names down."

"That's progress!" She turned and gave Louise a once-over. "*Look* at this little bitty girl. Come here, Louise." She laughed. "I can't call you just Louise. You got a nickname?"

"No," she lied. When her younger sister was learning to write, she spelled Louise "Louse" by accident and her father took "Louse" up enthusiastically. From then on it was one hated nickname after another. Louse became Mouse, Mousey, Lose, Loser, Loose 'n' Easy.

"They ever call you 'Weezy'?" said Mary.

"Nah. Sometimes 'Lou,'" she lied again.

Mary jumped up and encircled Louise's waist with her long fingers. "See that! I can get my hands around her whole waist. Girl, you are teeny! I wish I had those little dainty bones."

To hide her embarrassment and pleasure, Louise changed the subject to the difference between Myrtle Flynn and Mrs. Johnson. Both white ladies, but different as night and day.

"Maybe Mrs. Johnson should room with Mrs. Flynn," she said. "She'd have company, and Myrtle would be a good influence on her manners." Ardyce let some seconds go by before she replied.

"My advice to you," she said finally, "is don't get attached—"

"I'm not attached—"

"—'*cause* in the first place, they gonna die on you, or either they gonna be sweet to your face, and just when you get soft on 'em, they be talking evil. 'Nigger' this, 'colored' that, like that Parker, you heard her. And remember if they wasn't laid up and helpless, *outside* this place they be crossing to the other side of the street when they see *you* coming. My advice, just do your job right, so no one can complain about you, but don't expect nothing from 'em."

"No, now me, I'm the opposite," said Mary. "I see them laid up like that and I think, well *that* has evened things up for sure, *if* anybody's keeping score. 'Cause you can see they're suffering, and it's a terrible way to go out, all alone in a place like this. I don't care if they were, most of 'em, pretty well off. I feel sorry for them. Maybe it's just because I'm taking care of them, but I can't help myself, I *like* them. Even the ones I *know* I wouldn't like outside. And you can never know what they've been through in their lives. I give 'em the benefit of the doubt."

Ardyce grumbled, "'I doubt the benefit of the benefit of the doubt,' my mother used to say."

Mary turned to Louise, "And I don't mind if they sometimes drop their little words. Don't let that bother you, Weezy. My great grandmother lost her mind when she was old, called her own *grand*kids nigger. You can't be held responsible for what you say when you're senile."

Then Mary told a funny story. She said, "I was taking care of Great Grandma before she died, and she would soil herself at night, so I went over there to stay and I'd get up to change her. And there she'd be, two, three in the morning, sitting up in bed talking away with her dead sister—seeing her just as plain as day—had her arms stretched out in front of her like she was holding Auntie Edna's hands, talking kind of sweet and quiet, maybe comforting her about something. And I come in and say, 'Hi, G. G.,' and she says 'Hi, honey, just set down and have something to eat, honey.' And

I take off her gown and she raises her arms over her head to help me, and then I ask her could she lie down so I could change her linens, and she says, "Okay, thank you, honey," and she lays down just as nice. And after I strip the bed, I wipe her off and of course I had to wipe her private parts and put a little powder on 'em or she'd get a rash, and just when I go to put that powder down there, she yells out, 'Get your hands outta my pussy!'"

Ardyce shrieked. Laughing, Mary continued. "'Get your hands outta my pussy!' she says as loud as all get out. They could hear her halfway up the block. This refined little old lady who wore white gloves with lace edges to church every Sunday—never used bad language a day in her life until she lost her mind. See, that's why I say you can't hold them accountable." Mary wiped her eyes.

Ardyce said, "Well, your *own* is different, in my opinion."

"You like Myrtle Flynn, though, don't you, Ardyce?" asked Louise.

"Oh, she's a *love*!" said Mary.

"Flynn was a farm woman, so she know how to work, I'll say that for her. But I can't speak for her views."

At 2:30 the nurse sent Louise and Ardyce to check again on a wiry, combative little woman, who would be, as Ardyce put it, "Swimmin' in shit." Cora could be heard all the way down the hall, jabbering a mile a minute at the top of her lungs.

"What'd they feed this one? Just goes in one end, out the other," Ardyce grumbled. Louise was starting to get a headache and didn't reply but went to the bathroom and dampened two washcloths, remembering the routine from the night before. "Hold on to her! Don't let her loose!" Ardyce warned. "I don't want them mucky hands in my face!"

They wrestled her into a wheelchair and, with a sheet, tied her in under the armpits as she kicked her legs stiffly out in front. Louise blocked the wheelchair with her body so Ardyce couldn't see her fumbling to figure out which knob or lever would unlock the wheels. She pressed on two or three before accidentally hitting the right one. Then they rolled the little woman into the shower stall, where they took off her gown and grabbed her under each arm. She dug in her heels and tried to clutch on to a towel bar.

"*You* do it this time," Ardyce said pointedly. "I'll go hose down the chair," and she pushed the chair into the other shower room, leaving Louise alone with Cora. Cora began twisting and pulling her wrist until Louise, almost losing hold of her, in a panic, accidentally turned the water on full force. When the cold water struck Cora's back, she smacked Louise across the chest, then grabbed her around the neck, trying to pull herself out. Wet up to the elbow, Louise reached past her and clutched at the spigot handle again, turning the water warm.

Cora stood stock still and struck a pose for some seconds, the warm water streaming down her bare back and shoulders. Then she turned her face into the spray, puckered her lips, and blew out joyful sputterings, blinking the water off her lashes. Tentatively Louise loosened her grip on her and, finding Cora able to stand on her own, held her with only the tips of her fingers and washed her off gingerly with a soapy washcloth, trying not to get wetter than she already was.

Ardyce returned with the wheel chair and laughed. "You look like a drowned rat!" she said to Louise. After inspecting Cora's fingernails and hair, she shut the water off abruptly. "That's good. You're clean now, ain't you, Cora?" Bundling her into towels, they pushed her down into the wheelchair and tied her in again. On the way to her room, Cora thrust out her legs and arms and yelled: "GO BACK GO BACK GO BACK . . ."

The ringing bell shocked Louise awake. She had been dozing and dreaming, and she woke feeling guilty. In the dream she had been fired when Ardyce told them she couldn't balance Mrs. Johnson on her lap. Then, somehow she and her sister had custody of Mrs. Johnson and were trying to hide her from their father.

For a few seconds after the bell wakened her, Louise stayed where she was, continuing to rest her head in the crook of her arm, which was by now numb and tingling.

She lifted her head to look across the hall at the nurse asleep at the counter, her head cushioned by her sweater, and at the two aides sleeping upright on sofas in the darkened lounge. Ardyce stirred and opened an eye, but she made no move to get up and answer the bell. The harsh fluorescent lights made Louise's eyes water. She had her knife-in-the-eyes headache. The bell sounded again.

Moonlight filtering through the blinds streamed across a pair of knees rising and falling rhythmically, under the bed covers. The face was in shadow, but she remembered from last night how it would look, and waited in the doorway before going in.

After a moment, she went over to the bed and gazed down at the forehead that was drawn up into deep lines of distress.

"What do you need, Mrs. Freeman?"

"The pain . . . It hurts so," said the woman. Her knees went up and down, up and down, and her fingers worried the blanket.

"Do you want a pain pill?" She nodded. Louise turned to go, but Mrs. Freeman called her back.

"Get her to give you the *strong* kind. The gray and orange capsules. Not aspirin; that won't do me any good. You might as well not bring me anything at all if you bring that weak stuff. All right? … All right? Did you hear?" Louise slipped out the door without answering.

As soon as Louise touched the nurse's shoulder, she opened her eyelids heavy with green eye shadow.

"Hmm?"

"Mrs. Freeman wants a pain pill."

With a sigh, the nurse lifted her large frame from the creaking vinyl chair, and, pulling keys from her pocket, plodded over to the medicine closet.

"And she said she wants the gray and orange ones … She's in a lot of pain."

The nurse turned a cold eye on her.

"She *had* her pills tonight. She takes too much of that stuff and pretty soon it won't do her any good."

The nurse dropped two aspirin tablets from a large bottle into a small paper cup. Louise's headache was throbbing. She placed her palms on her temples and squeezed. Mary had wakened and was watching her drowsily.

"Got a headache?" she said.

"Yeah."

Mary reached for her pocketbook and pulled out a plastic pill box full of colorful pills—pink, blue, yellow and tan. She picked out a pink one and handed it to Louise.

"It's Darvon—double strength. That'll get rid of your headache in twenty minutes," she said, and laid her cheek back against the arm of the couch.

"Thanks a lot," Louise said, astonished at her generosity. Thanks didn't seem enough. "I'll pay you back," she said. Mary waved her away and closed her eyes.

At the drinking fountain Louise took the pill and remembered the little paper cup with Mrs. Freeman's aspirin, still on the counter. From down the hall she could hear the woman whimpering. She picked up the cup and carried it to her room.

"Here are your pills," Louise said. The old woman pulled herself up painfully and took the tablets in her trembling fingers. She dropped her hand into her lap, lay back and closed her eyes, tears oozing out from under her lids and sliding down around her ears.

Louise watched her for a moment without expression, and then turned to leave. Mrs. Freeman called her back.

"Wait!"

Louise poised in the doorway with one hand on the doorknob and one foot in the hall.

"Wait ... Could you at least rub my legs with lotion? They hurt so."

Louise stared dully at the moonlight shining through the half open blinds. The knife between her eyes dug deeper. She had no idea how to go about rubbing the pain out of the woman. The thought of putting her hands on those dry, ceaselessly moving legs repulsed her.

"I can't, I gotta answer another bell," she lied. "Try to sleep." She turned and hurried back down the hall. Passing the nurse's station, she slipped into the ward room like a fugitive, where she stood awhile in the dark. Myrtle was asleep, but it was enough just to be in the same room with her, where 'Who's that pretty little thing!' still rang in her ears. After a few minutes, she felt better and came out.

In the lounge, where the others continued to doze, Louise went to the magazine rack and picked out a greasy dog-eared, *Saturday Evening Post* she had already looked at twice. She set it down beside her on the couch and leaned her head back, thinking it had to be too soon for the Darvon to be taking effect, but feeling, even so, that her mood was just that moment beginning to change. The light snoring of her sleeping companions sounded comfortable and homey.

She thought about the apartment in the Lorelei and the bed with four throw pillows on a rose-printed bedspread and a ruffle around the bottom, everything rose, green and lavender. It wasn't a set—each one bought separately from the Goodwill and the Salvation Army stores—but they looked just right together. On both sides of the bed was a white bed table, one with a radio alarm and a *Reader's Digest* on it, the other holding her green cat mug and black satin sleeping mask.

Even though the Murphy bed could spring back into the wall leaving more space in the room, she liked to keep it down, made up neatly and decorated with the pillows overlapping.

It would be warm when she walked into the room, the sputtering radiator too hot to touch. She would be greeted by her pictures: a place called "Mont St. Michel" like a castle from a fairy tale, another with two horses galloping across a green valley below snowcapped mountains, and a photograph of her grandmother.

After her shift, she would be back there under the covers with her throw pillows stacked neatly on the one chair, her uniform soaking in the sink and her white shoes side by side on the closet floor. How quiet it would be sleeping in her own apartment—more than a room, because there was a separate bathroom and an alcove with a half-sized refrigerator and a hot plate. All the other apartments belonged to old and middle-aged people, church-goers who never yelled or threw things at each other but quietly went about their business, shopping or coming downstairs to take out the trash or going to work in the morning and coming home in the evening—mail carriers, beauticians, church deacons, retired railroad workers—people who kept their small apartments clean and their doors shut, who acted their age, like regular adults, paying their bills and watching television quietly with the volume low.

The battleground of home seemed so far away it must be in a different city. The apartment would be her home forever.

Warmth began to fill her body, spreading down her legs and arms. She smiled and closed her eyes but didn't feel sleepy, just loose and relaxed. For several minutes she sat, contented with the dimly lit lounge, the glimpse of exit lights down the hall, the contact between her hand and the cool plastic of the couch.

When another bell rang, she rose and walked dreamily down the corridor to a doorway where she could make out the figure of Miss Cowan, propping herself feebly on one elbow and clutching the bell cord. Louise went directly to her bed and laid a hand on her shoulder.

"I'm so wet!" cried the deaf old woman. "I tried to hold it, but I just couldn't. I'm sorry." Miss Cowan had luminous white hair, and cheeks so rosy that even in the dark you could make out their color. Louise petted her arms and stroked her head. Gently and slowly, she changed the bed, and the old woman lay back and let herself be cared for.

Louise sat by her bedside for a few minutes after finishing, and held her hands in her own. Miss Cowan smiled into her eyes.

"You're a dear, sweet girl. You're an angel of mercy," she said, and kissed her hands.

Louise leaned against the wall in the dark place in the corridor between the light from the exit sign at one end and the fluorescent glow from the nurse's station in the middle. It was 3:30, an hour and a half before second rounds. She could stand here and do nothing until then if she wanted to. Mary or Ardyce could answer the bells; she had already taken their turns at least once, trying to get in their good graces before her inexperience aggravated even Mary.

If someone did ring a bell, though, she wouldn't mind. At this moment she was starting to feel confident that whatever was asked of her she would be able to do. She pictured Mrs. Freeman's knees—outlined by the light coming through the blinds—rising and falling, rising and falling. She regretted that she hadn't massaged her legs.

Louise's headache had completely disappeared by now. Her heart fluttered a little from the drug, but pleasantly, the way it feels just before you know you're going to see someone who loves you, like her grandmother when they used to visit her in the country down in Alabama.

It occurred to her that she could go in and massage Mrs. Freeman's legs.

She crossed the hall and quietly entered the room, standing for a moment to listen.

There was no sound—not the rustling of sheets going up and down, or even the rhythmic sound of breathing. Louise tiptoed over to Mrs. Freeman's bed and bent close to look at her. The muscles in the old woman's face were drawn up as if she were protecting her eyes from bright lights, and her breathing was so shallow that Louise wasn't sure if she was asleep. To find out, she spoke to her in a whisper.

"Mrs Freeman … Do you want me to rub your legs now?" But the woman's hearing aid had fallen on to her pillow. Reaching out to touch her, Louise stopped mid-air, afraid of waking her just when she'd finally drifted off. She wished she had helped the woman while she'd had the chance. She was stricken with sadness, as if it were she herself who had been forced to make do with aspirin for a pain so crushing it made her grimace in her sleep.

Out in the corridor Louise wondered who else might be needing help. Mrs. Johnson's last words as she and Ardyce had left her room came back to her now, the ones that had been thrown away on them: "There's a lump in my blanket." In school, Louise had once, to her great surprise, been cast in a play. She had only one line, a 'throw-away line,' the teacher called it, meant to be ignored. "There's a lump in my blanket." Louise suddenly remembered the shaky cry that had delivered the line, and felt uneasy about it.

By her watch, she saw it was 3:45. How long was it since they'd walked away from Mrs. Johnson's cracked open door? About 1:45, she guessed. Two hours and forty-five minutes. There were only two rounds a night—one starting at 1:00, the other at 5:00. But they wouldn't get to Mrs. Johnson's end until at least 5:30. Between rounds they answered bells, but Mrs. Johnson couldn't ring her bell. "Don't we check on her in between?" Louise had asked on the first night. "No," said Ardyce sharply. "Johnson sleeps good and there's a catheter in her. If we go in there between rounds and wake her up, she'll have us on our feet all night, doing this, that and the other thing."

Louise couldn't get the lump in Mrs. Johnson's blanket off her mind. She imagined it pressing into the heavy, inert upper arm in that spot below the armpit that can send the pain all the way down to the inside of the wrist. She knew it very well. It was where her father got hold of her and pressed when he was in a mood. She could imagine a lump there becoming like a red hot stone until finally the whole arm would be burning like a cooked sausage ready to split.

She walked back up the hallway to the nurse's station where the nurse was now behind the counter doing charts. Mary and Ardyce were still asleep in the lounge. You weren't supposed to lie down on duty, but as long as you had one foot on the floor, you were okay. And anyway, the nurse slept, too.

I could go check on Mrs. Johnson right now, Louise thought, when no one would see me go. Just run in there and quickly move the arm. But what if Ardyce was awake when she came back and saw her coming from the south end; there was nothing down there to excuse her—the restroom was here by the lounge, the drinking fountain next to the nurse's station.

Maybe she could say she'd answered a bell. But Ardyce didn't sleep through bells, even if she only opened one eye and used it to stare Louise into getting up and answering it. She'd say, "*What* bell? I didn't hear no bell."

She walked softly over to the game table and sat down on a molded plastic chair that she knew wouldn't creak. She considered whether Mrs. Johnson was worth the worry. Not so much as a please or thank you from the woman. She was rude and probably a bad woman too. You could tell from her tough old cigarette voice and high society language.

She stood up. Checking to see if the nurse was paying attention, she eased out of her line of sight and started down the hall to the south end.

Halfway down the darkened hall she stopped. What if Mrs. Johnson asked to be turned and she had to say she couldn't turn her by herself? She might insist that she go get someone to help her.

Maybe Mary would be willing to come down and help if this happened. But Mary would tell her what she'd told her the night before: "It's fine and good to want to do extras for these patients, but they're going to want you to keep it up. The more you do, the more they want."

"But … Aren't we s'posed to take care of them?" Louise had asked, timidly, and Mary's kind eyes had turned chilly. She had taken her friendly hand from Louise's shoulder, folded her arms across her chest, and said, "That's fine for you, Miss Angel of Mercy. You can go home and get your sleep in that nice apartment you talk about. Sleep all day, if you want to.

"I got kids at home. I got to get the big ones to school and pick 'em up later, get the shopping done, keep the babies with me. When am I going to sleep if I can't catch a nap here at work? Where else am I going to get a job where I can take care of my kids? And Ardyce, she cannot be on her feet that much. She doesn't say it, because she needs to keep this job 'til she can go on social security, but every time she walks down that hall, her legs and feet swell up. You start doing this, doing that, pretty soon you make a load for the rest of us we can't handle."

After speaking her piece, she had softened again: "Girl," she said, "you want to be a help to these patients, just be nice. Give them a smile instead of a frown. Treat them with respect, but don't go messing with the schedule, now."

* * *

Louise approached Mrs. Johnson's room hesitantly, still not sure what to do. She pictured the woman's eyes open and expressive, trapped above the immobilized body. Maybe she ought to at least go in and see if Mrs. Johnson looked all right. She was probably asleep anyway. The door was ajar. She reached out her hand to push it open and immediately, as her arm cast a shadow across the crack, Mrs. Johnson called out.

"Nurse?"

Louise quickly pulled her hand back and stood against the wall, listening.

"Nurse! … Nurse! … Nurse!…"

Louise thought about the lump in the blanket. How could Mrs. Johnson feel the lump if she was paralyzed? Maybe it *was* just a throw-away line, an excuse to get more attention. She could have been the type of person before she got sick that sat around with her society friends bad-mouthing people and complaining about little things.

Louise's headache was returning. She wondered if it would be possible to talk Mary into another Darvon to take home. On tiptoe in her rubber-soled shoes, she backed away from Mrs. Johnson's door and took a few steps down the hall toward the light.

A strange sound stopped her. For a moment she had the un-likely thought that it was a kitten mewing, and looked around for one. The sound came again, higher this time. It was coming from Mrs. Johnson's room. Louise stepped back softly to the threshold of the door. Was Mrs. Johnson crying? Crying all alone, unable even to blow her nose? In her smock pocket she found a tissue and grasped it tightly. The sound came again, on a quavering, experimental note.

Mrs. Johnson had been finding her key, and now, in a rusty, late night soprano began to sing.

"Taking a boat to O-ma-ha,
Getting a cab to France,
Riding the rails to Ha-wa-ii,
That's how you find romance."

It was a jazzy, old-timey tune, the kind Louise's parents used to sing when she was small and they were still together.

"Doing it the hard way, hard way,
Doing it the ha-a-ard way,
So you haven't got a chance.

Going down to the hm hm hm,
da da da da the dance ... "

She stopped. Louise could hear her catching her breath, then coughing a little. It reminded her of how her littlest sister used to sing to herself in bed at night, nonsense words that made Louise laugh and feel better. Tears rose up behind Louise's eyes, filling the place where the headache pain was. She pulled the tissue out of her pocket and in doing so, caught a pen that was hooked on her pocket flap. It flipped onto the floor with a clatter.

"Nurse?"

It was impossible to stay here any longer. She had to either leave or go in and look after the woman. She began to edge away.

The voice started up again:

"Little Miss Tiptoe,
Who could she be?
Comin' like a mouse
To check on me.

Little Miss Tiptoe,
Standin' in the hall,

Can't be Mary 'cause
She's too tall."

There was a pause. Louise waited to see what would come next.

"Wouldn't be Ardyce,
She wouldn't come at all."

Louise heard a self-satisfied snort.

"Couldn't be the nurse,
'Cause her shoes do squeak.
Little Miss Tiptoe,
Can't you speak?"

Another pause.

"Tell me your name,
Oh, won't you please?
Is Little Miss Tiptoe
Miss Louise?"

Louise felt the skin on her arms prickle. She remembered what Mrs. Parker had said about meeting Mrs. Johnson in the hall. She pictured her standing upright and facing her, on the other side of the door. She pushed it open and switched on the light. Mrs. Johnson was still on her right side, just as they had left her.

"I came to straighten out the lump in your blanket," said Louise. "Is it bothering you?"

"Yes, it's bothering me. It feels like my arm is hatching an egg." Louise went around to the other side of the bed.

"I knew that was you. I could tell by your walk." Mrs. Johnson's face looked white and strained. Louise picked up her arm and smoothed out the blanket. "May I have a drink of water?"

Louise poured some into the glass, held it to her face and carefully put the straw between her lips. Mrs. Johnson sucked on the straw until the water was gone.

"How's your hip feeling?"

"It's fine. But the one I'm lying on is giving me fits now."

"Well, I'd like to help you, but—"

"You can't turn me by yourself."

"Maybe I could try—"

"No, you don't know how to do it. And you can't get help." She looked at her clock. "There's still about an hour and a half to wait."

"What were those songs you were singing?"

"Just a little thing or two to pass the time."

"Did you make them up?"

"I did indeed."

"How do you know how to do that?"

"I was a song writer. I used to make my living that way, such as it was."

"Really?"

"Don't you ever make up songs?" Louise shook her head. "Or stories or poems?"

"I'm not the creative type, I guess."

"Or pictures in your mind?"

"Not really."

"You *must* create *something*. Didn't you ever create a meal or a room or a conversation?"

Louise considered this.

"I created a room."

"Me too. See my dressing room? I'm just lying here on my couch until curtain time. The celebrated soprano, relaxing before going on. I'm so relaxed my whole body is completely still. I can't feel a thing." She smirked. "Preparation for my big role."

"How can you still feel your arm or your hip, Mrs. Johnson, when you're numb?"

"Are you asking if I'm numb or are you asking if I feel?" Louise didn't answer. "There're safety pins in my drawer there. Get one out." Louise opened the drawer. "Open up the pin and go into the bathroom; they've got some alcohol and cotton balls in there. Bring them here and wash that pin and the bottom of my foot with alcohol and stick the pin in my foot."

Louise's mouth dropped.

"I can't do that."

"Yes, you can. And I want you to. Go ahead … go on!"

Louise found the alcohol, came back and stood warily at the end of the bed.

"Pull the sheet back off my feet."

She pulled it back. Mrs. Johnson's feet were dry and puffed like overcooked potatoes, the toes blobs of flesh into which the toenails had burrowed deep.

"Are you doing it yet?"

"No."

"Do it."

"I don't think I should."

"All right then, don't."

Louise stood, undecided, with the pin poised over the foot. Curiosity got the better of her. She swabbed the foot and the pin with alcohol and delicately touched the point of the pin to Mrs. Johnson's sole. There was no response, not the slightest jerk. She pressed it in lightly, feeling some resistance and then a tiny pop as the skin gave way and the pin entered.

She looked back at Mrs. Johnson's face, which was composed. The safety pin stuck out of the flesh, as if the foot were a pin cushion. It was like something from a horror movie.

Quickly she pulled the pin out. A drop of blood welled up, a deep, satin red, brilliant against the white, powdery skin. Louise cleaned the blood with the cotton ball.

"Are you doing it?" said Mrs. Johnson, opening her eyes.

"I did it."

She took the safety pin and the swab into the bathroom and threw them in the wastebasket. She came back and drew the blanket up again.

"I can feel some things and not others," said Mrs. Johnson as Louise carefully smoothed the blanket and replaced the arm.

"What all *can* you feel?"

"I feel anything that I know will hurt me," she replied. "Neglect and where that will lead, a lump in a blanket pressing, the red spot on my hip—such things as that. Impatience, selfishness, contempt, dishonesty. I feel those." Tears suddenly slid down the side of her face. Louise stared at the box of tissues on the bedstand inches from the woman's face. "Tell me about your room," said Mrs. Johnson, as if the tears had not happened.

"What room?"

"The one you created."

"Oh … It's nothing. Just an apartment. It's quiet."

"You like that?"

"Uh huh … Do you want me to wipe your nose?"

With that, Mrs. Johnson's tears spilled over. She said in a choking voice, "Yes, you can wipe my nose. You can wipe my nose." Louise knelt by the bed so that their faces were at the same level. She put the fingertips of one hand on Mrs. Johnson's now flushed cheek and held a tissue gently up to her nose with the other.

"You sure are a good song writer," she said.

"Thank you." Mrs. Johnson blew her nose. "Was your heart breaking at the time?" she said, after a moment.

"At what time?"

"When you created the apartment?"

"Oh. No, I just wanted to get away."

"That's what *songs* are for. If your heart's been broken, a song will put it back together."

"I'm sorry I can't turn you by myself," Louise said. "I don't really know how." Mrs. Johnson was trying to clear her throat of the phlegm that her crying spell had produced, and didn't reply. "When I've been here longer I'll be able to turn you by myself."

At last Mrs. Johnson said, "Yes, you'll get the hang of it pretty soon. Pay attention to that Ardyce. She knows what she's talking about." Her eyes went to the clock. "They'll be starting second rounds soon. You'd better get back."

Louise stood up. She hesitated for a moment, and then pressed the catch on the bedrail and lowered it. She put a hand on Mrs. Johnson's shoulder and hip and tugged at them.

"Don't!" said Mrs. Johnson. "You might hurt yourself. You don't want to end up like me." Louise backed off and stood with her hands at her sides. Mrs. Johnson's voice became artificially cheerful. "I'm used to waiting, and I've got plenty of songs to help me pass the time. Why don't you just give me another sip of water before you go."

"Yeah, I don't think I could turn you without hurting you. Ardyce showed me three times already, but I can't remember." She picked up the water glass. "I was a dummy in school, too. Nothing stuck."

"Well, hold on. Just a minute. The trick is you've got to get your whole body into it."

"I know. I know."

"Not just your arms."

"But I don't know what that *means!*"

Mrs. Johnson narrowed her eyes as if she were coming to a decision.

"Get that extra pillow off the chair. I'm going to show you how to turn me."

Louise held the water glass out in the air. "But don't you want this drink?" she said.

"Afterwards."

"I can't do it," Louise protested. "I'm too weak."

"No, you aren't. Come on and bring the pillow here." Louise put the water glass down, reluctantly walked over to the chair and fetched the pillow. "All right," Mrs. Johnson said. "Now put it against my upper back and head. Lengthwise. Wedge it in a little. Not too much." Louise did as she was told. "Now pull the covers all the way off me."

Louise peeled the covers down across Mrs. Johnson's mountainous hip and thigh and bared the white bloated flesh of her calf, releasing a fusty smell of stale secretions and antibacterial soap. She waited at the foot of the bed, not wanting to touch her again.

Mrs. Johnson said, "Come back over here and put your knee up on the mattress right up against my waist."

Reluctantly, Louise came around to the side and, hiking up her white skirt, put one knee on the bed.

"Now you're going to put your right hand on my shoulder and your left hand on my hip and roll me into your knee. Just take it slow and easy."

Louise pulled and felt the huge bulk begin to roll toward her matchstick leg. For a moment she panicked and almost pulled her knee away.

"Slowly, slowly! Brace my shoulder with your chest, so you can let me down gently.

Step by step Mrs. Johnson explained how to bring her head and knees along as she turned, and how to use the pillows to keep her extremities from moving too fast. A bead of sweat dropped off Louise's forehead onto Mrs. Johnson's throat.

"Breathe," said Mrs. Johnson. "A held breath will steal all your strength."

Louise took in a small breath and let the air escape from her nose. It fluttered the wispy bangs on Mrs. Johnson's forehead.

"Take a much deeper breath than that," she said. "Listen, one time I had a screaming headache, but I had to go somewhere. And I got in my Rambler and turned the radio on. It was playing an aria from Aïda. And I started singing." Here she began to sing in her thin, hoarse soprano …

> "O terra, addio, addio valle mi pianti
> Sogno di gaudio che in dolor svani …

… only I wasn't pulling my punches like this, I was really belting it out. There was nobody to hear me except that straight highway. I hit the top notes like a diva! And when that aria was over, my headache was gone and the speedometer said ninety-five miles an hour. It was the breath. I'm telling you—*breathe!*"

Now Mrs. Johnson's legs were bent and partly spread eagled, the catheter tube snaking out from her private parts. That, more than her immobility or her lack of sensation forced on Louise an unwanted rush of pity.

With a few more maneuvers, she had Mrs. Johnson turned onto her back. She took another deep breath. The armpits of her uniform were wet. Now, seeing Mrs. Johnson's body stretched out flat like that, Louise experienced a moment of pride.

Mrs. Johnson turned her head to look at her. "You can stop for a minute."

Louise glanced at her watch. In fifteen more minutes Ardyce would expect the cart to be ready for second rounds. She said, anxiously, "Do you want to stay on your back and keep off that red spot for the rest of the night?

"No, I don't, because I'll be sitting on my duff strapped in a wheelchair all day, and my bottom needs an airing at night. I'm like a big shishkebob—you have to keep turning me till I'm done evenly on all sides. Let's finish this thing. Are you ready? Here's where you have to be very careful of your back. I'm 257 pounds of dead weight the last time they put me on a scale, and you're going to have to slide my whole body over toward the right side of the bed so when you turn me onto my left side I'll end up in the middle and not on the floor with a cracked skull. Go around to the other side."

Louise didn't move. "My arms are pretty weak," she said.

"You can do it if you listen to what I tell you. Take the draw sheet and the fleece and roll them up tightly against my side, a long roll you can get your hands around." Louise went around and rolled the bedding. "Ready? You're going to get in real close again, put your knee up and pull on me by the draw sheet. Louise reached out and, grasping the roll, yanked it backwards.

"No, no. Not with just your arms. Have you ever put a big piece of furniture on a throw rug and moved it across the room pulling it by the rug? It's the same principle. You've got to use your whole weight."

"But that's on a slick floor—this is a mattress."

"I know. That's why you have to get in very close to me, put your knee up on the bed again, get your forehead right down on my stomach and pull with your elbows in to your sides, like before. Lie with your thigh up against your chest and then let your rear end pull your body backward as you pull me."

Louise got into position and with only the thin layer of Mrs. Johnson's hospital gown between them, lay with her face on the great cushion of her stomach. As her cheek touched the fabric, she remembered pressing her face against her mother's belly, full with her sister, the sister's beating heart, her kick—so long ago that the memory came and went without a name for it, just a sensation, but it did something to ease her fear.

With palms up, she curled her fingers under the rolled sheet, grasped it tightly, and pulled. It was like trying to move a car with the brakes on. Nothing budged.

She sat back. "I can't *do* it."

"Yes, you can. I know you can." Tears pricked Louise's eyes, but she blinked them away. "Calm down and try again."

She got in closer in a tight crouch, at the same time letting her pelvis, the center of her weight, pull back off the bed so that her body hung from the points where she grasped the sheet. As she pulled again, she took in a lungful of air and puffed it out like a woman in labor and felt Mrs. Johnson slide toward her a fraction of an inch. She pressed herself closer into her own knee and pulled again slowly and steadily, her biceps hardening in her skinny upper arms as Mrs. Johnson's body began to inch steadily, ponderously toward her, dragged by her counterweight.

"That's it. You've got it. Go a couple more inches."

Amazingly, Louise's arms seemed to be getting stronger, Johnson's body lighter as it inched across the bed. Louise felt muscular, like a man. She wanted to just keep on pulling.

"That's it," said Mrs. Johnson. "You can stop."

"It was easy!"

"So now you can turn me onto my other side the same way you got me onto my back only in reverse. I'll tell you how."

Louise nodded. She rested her hand lightly on Mrs. Johnson's shoulder.

Mrs. Johnson said, "You're gonna get this old shishkebob cooked yet!"

"Done to a turn," said Louise. Mrs. Johnson laughed. Her laugh flooded Louise with an unfamiliar pride and sudden love. She imagined being Mrs. Johnson's private nurse. They would tell each other their life stories while Louise bathed her and dressed and fed her. At night they would lie awake together making up funny songs.

"What are you doing?!"

The nurse stood in the doorway staring at them with the look of a woman who has caught a cheating husband. Louise backed away from the bed.

"I was turning Mrs. Johnson," she said.

"Mrs. Johnson doesn't need turning yet."

Unable to move her head, Mrs. Johnson said to the ceiling, "I *told* her to turn me."

The nurse ignored her. To Louise she said, "We're trying to keep her off that bedsore."

"Well, Ardyce said it wasn't too bad, and Mrs. Johnson's other hip was bothering her—"

"Did Ardyce tell you to turn her?"

"No, ma'am."

"*I* told her to turn me." A tremor in Mrs. Johnson's jaw and pursed lips showed the effort she was making to get the nurse in her line of vision.

The nurse moved a little closer to the bed. "And how did you get this girl down here? Ring the bell, did you?"

Louise said, "I just thought it seemed like a long time since we checked her."

"How long was it? When did Ardyce finish rounds?"

Louise tried to think. What was it supposed to be, 2:00 or 2:30? She thought 2:30.

Rattled, she said, "2:00, I mean 2:30."

"Which was it?"

"I meant 2:30. It was 2:30."

"Did Ardyce hurry through them?"

"No. It just seems like a long time until 5:30 to be laying on one side like that and—"

"Mrs. Johnson doesn't always agree with us about her care, so you should check with me before you think about doing anything like this. She shouldn't be left on her back—"

"She was about to finish turning me onto my other side," Mrs. Johnson interrupted.

"This girl is too small. She shouldn't do it without help." The nurse glanced at her watch. "And I don't have the time; I've got to finish giving these meds." She turned to go. To Louise she said, "I'm going to send Ardyce down to finish this job you've got half done, and then you start your rounds." She moved out into the hall and over her shoulder said, "They keep hiring you kids off the street with no experience and then expect us to keep up standards. And *I'm* the one held accountable."

No longer able to see the nurse, Mrs. Johnson raised her voice. "Say, Mrs. Kretschmer, I want to thank you for the excellent job you and your night staff do here. I've been meaning to say something to administration about it. Ardyce taught Louise some good tips about turning me tonight since I'm kind of a special case. She picked it up very quickly. You want to show Mrs. Kretschmer what you learned, Louise?" Louise stepped forward and picked up a pillow.

"Not now," called the nurse. Then she gave a long, grudging sigh. "All right, go ahead and finish up here, but then get Ardyce and start your rounds." She pushed her medicine cart down the hall toward Mrs. Parker's room.

Ardyce was beginning to gather up the leftovers of her lunch and put the magazines back on the rack, and Mary was returning from answering a bell on the north end when Louise entered the lounge from the south wing. They both said simultaneously, "Where've *you* been?"

"The nurse send you for something?" asked Mary.

Lowering her voice, Ardyce, said, "That nurse runnin' you ragged? Where is she? What'd she *want*?"

"I don't know where she is. She didn't send me anywhere."

Ardyce raised her eyebrows. "Then what you been doing?"

Louise shrugged and took a drink from the drinking fountain. "Nothing," she said. "I went and turned Mrs. Johnson, that's all."

Mary and Ardyce stared at her.

"She rang her bell."

And as if it were a throw-away line, Louise ambled down the hall to get the cart ready for rounds.

Louise pushed open the Center's smoked-glass double doors and stepped out into fresh air. Frost glinted off the car hoods in the parking lot. Pink and lavender rays of early morning sun were fanning out behind a bank of slow moving clouds.

She hardly ever noticed such things, hardly ever lifted her nose above the level of traffic lights and store fronts. But this morning she saw everything as if she had just emerged from a cave. At the bus stop she was tempted to keep walking all the way back through the suburbs, across the vague dividing zone of gas stations and chain stores, on into the city. But the bus came and swept her up and took her home.

As usual, she walked the block from her stop, ran up the unpainted front steps of the house, past her older brother sprawled asleep on the couch in the living room, and went into the kitchen. An egg-encrusted plate and used coffee cup told her that her father had already eaten and left for work. By 8:00 she'd gotten the younger kids some breakfast and sent them off to school. She went into the bathroom and took off her uniform, washed it in the small sink, wrung it out and pushed aside some towels to hang it over the shower bar. She brushed her teeth and rinsed with water from her green cat mug that sat next to the sink.

When she was through, she walked down the narrow hall to the bedroom.

As usual her sisters hadn't made the bed. She pulled a lop-eared teddy bear from between the rumpled covers and tossed it on the floor. A rickety orange crate served as a bedside table. She took up the ragged dishcloth she kept on the crate, and climbed in between the sour sheets. For a while she lay looking at the small crescents of sunlight that came through rips in the window shades. Yesterday she had found it hard to fall asleep in the daytime.

She draped the dishcloth across her eyes and lay there thinking about her wages. Her first paycheck would come a week from Friday. She could keep only ten percent for herself. "If you're not in school, you're gonna pull your weight around here," her father told her. How long would it take to come up with a deposit and first month's rent on an efficiency apartment in that building? Lorelei. A fancy name. Did it even have efficiency apartments?

Two dollars and thirty cents an hour with the night differential, so eighteen forty a day. She'd started work on a Tuesday. So, what would that be? Four days plus five days … she couldn't do the math in her head. She was always bad at numbers. Trying to figure it out, she fell asleep with a thin ray of sun shining across her cheek.

Moth

I T'S AROUND quarter to nine, almost dark. He has to get out
of this concrete block shithole before he goes crazy. One room,
and a bathroom you can hardly turn around in. A hot plate on
a table stained with cigarette burns and old coffee cup rings. One
window. A rattling fan. What a joke, a *fan*, to push hot air at him.
Might as well be back in lock up. Except no, at least in his shithole
he can walk out the door whenever he wants. Not that there's
anywhere to go.

The door opens directly onto a broken sidewalk. A streetlight
shines down on the potholes and patches of old tar along the street.
On the other side is a vacant lot filled with construction rubble
and weeds.

For a few minutes he stands in the doorway and wonders what
to do with himself. He has no energy, but he needs to get out, go
somewhere, do something to get rid of the useless thoughts looping
around in his head. He thinks of those fifteen years daydreaming
about the moment when he would walk out the gate. If anyone
was watching, they'd see him saunter, with a straight posture, no
slouching, as if it was natural to him to be free.

What a moron he was. Who would be watching? No one from
inside, and no one from outside after fifteen years. If he'd talked
about this daydream with anyone inside, he would have embar-

rassed himself. He's embarrassed for himself right now, just thinking about it. Eighteen when he went in. So stupid he didn't know it was possible to die from a single Molly. Dehydrated from dancing all night. The pill heated her up. That's all he'd given her, one pill. He hardly even knew her. Just showing off: Look what *I* got.

Nobody to meet him. Nobody to call. They'd confiscated his address book when they brought him in and never gave it back. The phone numbers would be no good anyway. People move on. His half-sister was the only one who might have cared, if she hadn't got pissed at him for taking money from her purse. Regularly. Why would he have done that to her? Worthless piece of shit.

And fighting inside. Someone gives him some lip and bang, he's punched his way out of parole. Served the whole fucking sentence with no parole services on the other end. Nothing. On your own. Seventy three dollars and fifty-six cents of gate money, already gone for last week's rent, food, a few bus tokens. What'll he do for next week?

So far looking for work had been pointless. City sanitation, McDonald's, that body shop. He could tell they were going to rip up his application as soon as he walked out the door. If you say you have a record, you're fucked. If you don't, they'll find out on a background check and you'll still be fucked.

He tries to give himself a pep talk. He could get in a better mood, at least for tonight, if he could find a way to get high—just some weed, one joint. Mellow him out, get him through the night. And in the morning he could figure out what to do. But he has no money for weed.

Before he came out tonight, he shoved a pair of thin surgical gloves in his pocket, the ones he'd taken from a box at the hospital— AVOID SPREADING CONTAGION. PROTECT YOURSELF AND OTHERS. He only took them because they were free and he might as well get something out of the trip since they weren't hiring, at least nobody with a felony on their record. It wasn't that he had anything in mind to do with the gloves.

Finally he gets himself to move. He walks to the strip a block away, crosses the highway and starts up the sidewalk of a short street with apartment buildings on one side and run-down, one-story houses on the other.

Half a block away he notices a woman standing in the grass between the sidewalk and a building. At this distance and in the dark, he can't see her very clearly, but she has white hair, that he can see, and she's turned away from the street, standing a little bent. It looks like there's a purse with a strap across her chest.

It would be so easy to snatch that purse up over her head before she knew what was happening. No need to knock her down or some shit like that. He could streak down the hill afterwards and take a right between the buildings at the corner. Once he was far enough away, he would dig out the cash and dump the purse with the rest of it—credit cards, phone. His prints are in one of those data bases, and he's living in the neighborhood, but if he left no prints, there'd be nothing to match.

He takes the gloves from his pocket and pulls them on but stays where he is.

Am I really this stupid, he thinks as he watches the woman? After all those wasted years, to risk getting locked up again?

The woman doesn't seem to be moving. Maybe she's senile. She might not even *have* money in her purse.

Don't even think about it, he tells himself. Turn around and go back. Don't be a moron. But he can't stand the thought of another night in that hotbox alone with nothing and nobody to take his mind off himself.

Up and down the street, the windows in most of the apartments and houses are dark. In a few, the light shifts colors in the cracks around the shades—TVs on, probably turned up loud. Window air conditioners going. No one will hear anything happening outside, and her phone will probably be in her purse. By the time she gets anyone to pay attention, he'll be long gone.

He walks up the hill slowly. Timing will be important. He'll have to be sure there are no cars coming and her back is still turned.

Just as he starts to move, car lights come up and pass. He stops and turns his face away. Some seconds later another car passes. He waits a few more moments. The air is muggy and heavy. Sweat soaks his shirt.

Now he picks up his pace, and his heart starts to pound. Jesus, why am I doing this?

As he comes closer to her, he walks in slow motion on the balls of his feet, like a cartoon cat ready to pounce. I'm a cartoon character, he thinks, a fucking cartoon character.

He's almost behind her, only a yard away. If he doesn't do it now, there won't be another chance.

Moving too fast, he catches his toe on a jutting piece of sidewalk and lurches forward, scuffing his shoe against the concrete. She hears and turns. Her eyes are wide, her mouth open.

"Oh!" she cries. Suddenly she steps up and grabs him by his arm. Still off balance, he stumbles onto the grass. "Look!" she says. Drawing him closer to the building, she slides a black, square object from her purse. A subcompact pistol, he thinks, and backs off, trying to get a footing on the uneven ground. But she tugs him forward, close to a shadowy flower bed.

"Look down!" she says. "Can you see them? It's so exciting! I've never seen one before. I've read about them, but I've never seen one." She lets him go and raises the small camera and points it toward the flowers. The flash goes off. "They're Hummingbird Moths! Isn't that great?" She takes him by the arm. "You can come closer, they won't pay any attention to you. I think they're too busy getting drunk on nectar." Her face tilts up to his. Her sagging cheeks rise in a smile. "See 'em?"

He stares at where she's pointing but doesn't see anything in the dark.

Lightly, she puts her palm on the front of his damp T-shirt. "If you just stand still for a few seconds and watch, you'll see movement among the flowers. See? There's one." She points. "There's another. Oh, look, two more. Hummingbird Moths! Boy, they're out in force tonight."

He leans in and looks closer. Now he sees the shadowy moths just visible hovering among the flowers, taking their time at each one. Their wings are moving so fast they're a blur.

"With the flash, you can see them like daylight. Here," she says, holding up her camera. She presses a button to illuminate the screen. "Wait a minute. Let me go back." The picture she has just taken comes up. "This is a close-up."

The moth is big and fat compared to the flower. Brown and yellow stripes go in different directions all over its head and body. A splash of red decorates the striped wings, which the camera has caught, frozen in mid-flight.

"See that long skinny thing? Going into the flower? As thin as a hair? That's its tongue! Just like a hummingbird, isn't it? Have you seen hummingbirds up close?"

Where would he have seen a hummingbird? When he was a kid, before prison, he didn't pay attention to anything like that.

"Nah. I don't think so."

"Well, these moths look a lot like them," she says, conversationally. "If you give me your e-mail, I'll send you this photo."

"That's okay. But thanks."

"Well, if you want to see them again, they showed up around quarter to nine, and—what is it now?" She presses a button to light her watch face. "About 9:15. I wonder if this is it, or they'll stick around for a few days. I'm going to come back tomorrow night, weather permitting, and see if they're still here." She puts her camera in her purse. "Well, I'd better be getting home. Take care." She flutters her hand at him in a little wave good-bye. He nods. It's dark enough that she hasn't seemed to notice his gloves.

She steps onto the sidewalk and heads up the hill. He takes another look at the shadowy movement in the flower bed. After a few yards, she turns back and calls, "There's so much life going on at night that we never see. You have to keep your eyes and ears open." Abruptly, she looks up at the sky. "There!" she says. "Did you hear that? That screech? It's a nighthawk. If you wait a few seconds, you'll hear it again." She continues up the sidewalk.

He waits. A few seconds later he does hear it again. And again. And again. He looks up and can just make it out very high in the night sky, soaring, diving, and calling. For the moment, he's forgotten that he needed to get high tonight.

Acknowledgments

I FIND IT impossible to feel even mildly confident that a story is done until it has benefited from the suggestions and comments of several readers, the more the better. Many people helped me with these stories over the decades during which I was writing them, including not only astute readers but a few experts to check the accuracy of certain details (How many adult diapers might a person go through in a day? Is it possible to get pregnant from penetration of only an inch? What happens to a felon upon walking out of the prison door after serving a full sentence?) That's where it's handy to know a geriatric nurse, an ObGyn nurse, a prison psychologist, a probation officer, and Google. With all this help, I felt less insecure about subtle errors and wrong turnings and ready to bring *A Little Something for Everyone* into the light of day.

First and foremost I want to thank Caryl Lyons—skillful editor, discerning reader and constant friend—for reading and critiquing many of these stories several times and for her careful reading of the manuscript as a whole. Anna Mary Mueller kindly read the first proof and added her suggestions.

I am also grateful to the following people for helping me think about and shape and correct the stories in this collection: Lisa Beiwel, Madeline Bendorf, Patrick Butler, Jeanette Carter, Shirley Dickinson, Judi Gust, Jackie Harb, Claudine Harris, Niki Harris, Lorie Hill, Lucy Luxenburg, Brownie Runge, Marcia Smies, Nancy Sprince, Jean Walker, and Kim Webster.

KATE KASTEN, in an earlier phase of her life, wrote, performed and toured a solo act—*Kate Kasten Comedy Theatre*. After a decade of portraying eccentric characters on stage, Kasten switched to fiction and is now the author of four novels and two other short story collections. She lives and writes in Iowa City, Iowa.